FIRES
in the
Wilderness

FIRES
in the
Wilderness

A story of the Civilian
Conservation Corps Boys

JEFFERY L. SCHATZER

BIG BELLY BOOKS
P. O. Box 1127
Bellaire, MI 49615

www.bigbellybooks.com

PRINTED IN THE UNITED STATES OF AMERICA

Schatzer, Jeffery L.

Fires in the wilderness : a story of the Civilian Conservation Corps boys / Jeffery L. Schatzer. —Bellaire, MI: Big Belly Books, [2015], c2008.

pages ; cm.

ISBN: 978-0-9749554-2-1
First published in 2008 by Mitten Press.
Audience: ages 8-12.
Summary: This novel follows Jarek Sokolowski and some of his Polish American friends who worked for the Civilian Conservation Corps in Northern Michigan from April 1934 to August 1934; clearing land, fighting fires, and growing from boys into men.—Publisher.

1. Civilian Conservation Corps (U.S.)—Juvenile fiction. 2. Depressions—1929—Juvenile fiction. 3. Bullies—Juvenile fiction. 4. Wildfires—Juvenile fiction. 5. Polish Americans—Juvenile fiction. 6. Upper Peninsula (Mich.)—History—20th century—Juvenile fiction. 7. [Civilian Conservation Corps (U.S.)—Fiction. 8. Depressions—1929—Fiction. 9. Bullies—Fiction. 10. Wildfires—Fiction. 11. Polish Americans—Fiction. 12. Upper Peninsula (Mich.)—History—20th century—Fiction.] 13. Bildungsromans. I. Title.

PZ7.S338 .F57 2015   2015932407
[Fic]—dc23   1502

Cover illustration by Jeff Ebbeler

FIRES
in the
Wilderness

Through the 1930s, the Great Depression held an ugly grip on the United States. Millions of people were out of work and without money to purchase food, shelter, or clothing.

President Franklin D. Roosevelt established the Civilian Conservation Corps, the CCC, to fight the paralyzing depression and put young people to work. This program hired young men from across the United States and its territories to work on projects that improved the land and protected the environment. The money these boys earned helped their families purchase the food and shelter they so desperately needed.

Many of the first boys to enroll in the CCC came out of urban areas, trained at army camps, and shipped to wilderness areas in order to begin their work.

ONE

Skinny Cats

April 1934

MATKA (MOTHER) STOOD ON THE BACK PORCH LOOKING OUT
into the darkness. The dim light from behind her made it
look like she was glowing. Her housedress was frayed and
faded. The tattered apron over her dress bore stains of time
and mountains of Polish food. Her hands fumbled nervously
at the hem of her apron, twisting it into a knot.

"Jarek," she called out to me, "do not be gone long.
Tomorrow is big day for you and Sid."

"Yes, Matka," I replied. Though I wanted to run back to
her, it would be too hurtful. Good-byes had already been
said, another one would be even harder. Instead, I turned
back to the path. My eyes slowly adjusted to the dark as I

followed the rutted walkway that traveled from our back door to the alley. Clouds moved across the thin sliver of moonlight. The city was covered in a blanket of darkness. No matter, I knew every root and stone in the path. There was comfort in its imperfection, a comfort I would miss dearly.

The path ended at the alley. From there I followed wheel ruts that cut through the dirt. A few families on the block had automobiles, but the buildings that lined the alley housed mostly horses and carts. Since I was little, my buddies and I had been meeting in the alley just a few houses down from ours. It was one of the only places we had to share a bonfire, swap stories, and enjoy the company of friends.

A sudden movement in the night shadows startled me. A pack of skinny cats scurried down the alleyway, weaving back and forth down the dusty ruts. They scoured every doorway and trash can in a desperate search for food. Ribs poked out from skinny sides. Their legs moved in a blur as their noses tested the air. They would fight for the smallest morsel of food.

I felt like one of those skinny cats. This was 1934, and the world was suffering from the Great Depression. The money had long since run out. *Ojciec* (Father) had lost his job at the furniture factory. *Siostra* (Sister) and Matka had no work since the hotel closed. *Starszy Brat* (older brother) Squint and I lost our jobs at the wagon company downtown. There was no work to be found. Worst of all, food was scarce. Ojciec did not like taking handouts from the government, the church, or anyone. We made do as best we could with hand-me-down clothes and shoes.

It was our last night with our families in Grand Rapids for a long, long time. This was the last bonfire we would share with friends. Luck had run out. We were skinny cats running for our very lives.

I tried not to show fear. At least I would be with my friends and my *brat* (brother) at the meeting place in the alley—Yasku, Stosh, Pick, Squint. Though his given name is Sid, nearly everyone called him "Squint." His eyesight had been bad for as long as I could remember. Unfortunately, eyeglasses were a luxury that my *rodzina* (family) could not afford. He got his nickname because he squinted to see everything.

By the time I reached the meeting place, the bonfire was roaring. It would take the chill off the cool April night. Yasku Solinski scrounged some branches from a pine tree that had fallen over by St. Adalbert's Church on Fourth Street. The sap in the wood made loud popping and cracking sounds and sparks chased high into the sky. The dry pine burned fast and hot. A bed of coals shimmered in shades of orange and red. I rubbed my hands together and warmed them by the fire.

From down the alley, a window opened. Mr. Damski poked his head out. "You kids watch that fire. Don't burn the city down!"

Squint answered, "Yes sir, Mr. Damski, we'll be careful."

"Just make sure you got some water to douse that fire." The window slammed shut, and we all turned to Stosh.

Stosh Campeau lived the closest, so he left to fetch a bucket of water from the pump in his backyard. As he walked back with the full bucket, cold water sloshed against him with each step. Though his house was no more than thirty paces away, everything from his knees on down was soaking wet. Stosh put the bucket down next to the fire, then plopped himself onto a rock and took off his shoes and his pants. He placed his wet shoes next to the fire. Then he stood up and started drying his pants, waving them above the flames. Stosh didn't seem to give a second thought about being practically naked in the alley.

I covered my mouth to keep from laughing as I watched him. Stosh was always doing stupid stuff. Spilling water all over his legs was just another dumb thing he did. Steam started rolling off his pants as the water evaporated. After a time he put them on again. When he did, the pants were hot in a few spots. We all laughed as he hopped around, trying to cool off his steaming drawers.

After our laughter died down, I turned my attention to the bonfire. Fire seemed to have magical powers. Its sights, sounds, and smells fascinated me and caused me to think. As I stared into the flames and embers, I thought about the words Ojciec had spoken to Squint and me earlier. In broken English, he said, "My sons, to become a man is hard. For a boy to become a man is harder still. For what you will do, I am very proud." Warmth from the fire washed over me. In a while I would have to move around in order to warm my backside.

The wind shifted slightly. I turned my eyes away from the stinging smoke as Frank "Pick" Kowalski used a stick to push small potatoes around in the hot coals. Dinner was almost ready. For most of us, this would be the only meal of the day—one scrawny potato. It was a meal the skinny cats would have fought for.

"When are them spuds gonna be ready?" said Yasku as he rubbed his hands and warmed them by the fire. "I ain't et nothin' since yesterday."

"Hold your horses," Pick said. "We're all hungry." He poked around in the hot coals, pushing the potatoes onto a piece of scrap wood. "Let them cool or you'll burn yourself."

Stosh was putting a new piece of cardboard in his shoe to cover the hole in the bottom. We all knew that Stosh's shoes were older than he was. The soles had long since developed large holes. Since his family had no money for even secondhand shoes, Stosh resorted to putting cardboard over the holes from time to time. He inspected his work and smiled. "There, that ought to give me a few more miles." He slipped his shoe back on, careful to keep the cardboard in place. "Say, did ya hear that Mrs. Czpanski got a whole can of meat for cleaning some rich family's house?"

"Ya, I heard that her kids got a spoonful each for dinner," Squint said as he whittled a stick with his old pocket knife. He speared a potato before continuing. "Other than handouts from the state and a loaf of bread here and there, that's all they got to eat."

"I'm tired of being hungry all the time," Stosh added.

Pick took a bite of his potato. Steam floated off the white center. He used his hand as a fan, trying to cool the potato in his mouth. "I heard that when we get into the Civilian Conservation Corps, we'll get three hots and a cot."

"Huh?" Yasku asked. His mouth was stuffed with potato.

"You know," Squint chimed in. "Three hots and a cot ... three hot meals each day and a cot to sleep on at night."

"Three hot meals every day?" I asked. "No kidding?"

"Just a minute," Yasku began as he looked across the bonfire at me. "You ain't old 'nuff to join, are you?"

"I'll be sixteen next week."

"How'd you get in?" Yasku asked. "You got to be eighteen. And if I remember right, brothers ain't supposed to join at the same time."

I hung my head in silence. Squint raised up full and looked around. "I told the selection agent that he's my cousin—eighteen years old, just like me. Any of you say anything different, I'll knock your block off. Understand?" No one spoke another word.

Pick swallowed the last of his potato and broke the awkward silence. "It's chilly, even for April," he said looking into the fire. "Maybe where we're going it'll be nice. Bet ya there'll even be a lake where we can go swimming."

Much of that night we were lost in our individual memories, thoughts, and fears. A spring storm was moving in from Lake Michigan. Lightning danced off to the west as the sky grumbled with distant thunder. The skyline of the tired city lit up in brilliant flashes, only to be quickly swallowed up again by darkness.

"Lightning is like fire from the sky," said Stosh, gesturing toward the gathering storm. We nodded in agreement as we concentrated on the dance of the flames and the shifting colors of our own bonfire. As a light rain began, we doused the fire and scurried off like skinny cats to catch a few hours of sleep before leaving Grand Rapids, perhaps for good.

My stomach growled, begging for more food.

TWO

Train to Tomorrow

THE WEATHER CLEARED BY MORNING, AND WE STARTED OUT ON our adventures in the CCC, the Civilian Conservation Corps. The train left Grand Rapids and headed for Battle Creek with other boys our age. I'd guess there were about two hundred of us. A handful of paying passengers were sprinkled here and there. I sat next to Pick, facing Yasku, Stosh, and Squint.

Loud clanking, metal-on-metal sounds echoed through the terminal as the locomotive crept forward. Cars in the train clasped each other. The heavy wheels of the engine grabbed at the tracks and the chug of the engine slowly picked up a rhythm. When our car jerked to life, we held on to keep from being tossed in our seats. Voices rose in a collective "whoa" as a few loose items skittered across the floor. We cheered as the train gathered speed heading out of town.

Pick, Squint, Yasku, Stosh, and I spoke in Polish, sharing the excitement of our first train ride. Train yard dogs chased alongside us, their tongues hanging long from the corners of their mouths. We waved at people outside the window and joked amongst ourselves in the language of our neighborhood.

From behind us, someone spoke out a little too loudly: "Polacks." We all froze. It was a word that none of us liked because it was used to make fun of us, our language, and our families.

It was a word that could lead to a fight.

We all looked around to see who said it, but there was no way of telling. Some of the fun was stolen from our train ride.

"Let's not make trouble," Pick said. "We should speak English."

From that time on, we spoke English. Between us we agreed to speak Polish only when we were alone or when we wanted to keep something a secret. Though using English would help avoid some problems, it didn't feel right. Polish was the language that had been with me all my life. Speaking English felt like turning my back on my family.

Thoughts of home occupied our hearts and minds as the city got smaller in the distance. The sickly, bitter smell of coal smoke from the steam engine penetrated the car. A coating of greasy ash clung to everything. Still, nothing could take away from the pure excitement of the trip. None of us had been more than a few blocks from home ever before in our lives. Every mile of rail and every small town along the way was an adventure.

The rocking motion of the train eventually lulled me to

sleep. The strangest dream came to me. I was running away from something, something fearful. Its breath was hot on my shoulders. No matter how fast I ran, the beast kept gaining ground. It clawed at my back and roared in my ears. As the beast was about to consume me, I was jarred awake by a sudden jolt.

Pick elbowed me in the ribs and pointed to a fella who was handing out paper bags. Lunch was being served to the CCC boys. Each of us got an apple and a baloney sandwich slathered with butter and mustard. It had been a long time since any of us had been given a whole sandwich to eat. The apple was an added bonus.

"What kind of jobs do you think we're gonna do?" Yasku asked as he savored his lunch.

"Don't know," Squint said, wiping his mouth on his shirt sleeve. "Work is work. I don't much care as long as I have a job."

"Me, I want to drive a truck," I said between bites. "That's got to be the greatest job in the world."

As Squint was about to comment, an apple core flew out of nowhere and hit him smack on the side of the head. It splattered its sticky juice all over his face and onto his clothes. My brother shot up as a group of boys a few seats away broke out in laughter.

"Who threw that?" Squint demanded as he charged the jokesters.

"Who wants to know?" shot back the biggest one.

The big-mouthed guy stood up quickly, towering over Squint. They started exchanging words and began a shoving match. The once–noisy railcar got quiet as all eyes turned toward the ruckus. I didn't want to see Squint get into a tussle. My brother wasn't much of a fighter, though he was never one to back down.

Squint pushed off from the other guy and balled up his fists. "Put up your dukes, you punk!"

I scrambled out of my seat to break up the fight. Then it happened. I got between Squint and the big guy and pushed them apart. At the very same moment, the train car lurched violently. The big guy went tumbling down the aisle, head over heels. Squint and I managed to hang on and stay upright.

After regaining his balance, the big guy jumped to his feet and scrambled forward with fire in his eyes. Before he was on us, our buddies stood to back us up. His face was red with anger, but it was obvious that he didn't want to fight all of us. He pointed a finger at me. "Nobody, but nobody, pushes Big Mike O'Shea around."

"Knock it off," said one of the paying passengers. "Go back to your seats and pipe down." The passenger shook his newspaper in disgust before returning to his reading.

Mike O'Shea looked me up and down. "You and I will have it out one day."

"You'll have to go through me first, O'Shea," Squint responded. "You're the one who'll have to watch your step." Squint wiped the juice off his face with his shirt sleeve. "C'mon, it's over. Let's go back to our seats."

Big Mike looked around at Yasku, Stosh, and Pick before sitting down hard. I stared out the window once again and thought. Since we were little kids, Squint had always been the one who stood up for me. This was the first time I actually stood up for him. My heart swelled with pride. It felt good, very good.

I put Mike O'Shea out of my mind as the train clicked and clacked over the rails. We passed through mile after mile of barren farm fields and towns we'd heard of but never seen—Moline, Wayland, Plainwell, Kalamazoo, and others.

Encampments along the way, called hobo jungles, could be seen next to the tracks outside many of the cities. Those with nothing but a few meager possessions and the clothes on their backs gathered there. The tents and shacks in these run–down communities housed the poor as they looked for work or bummed for handouts from kind and generous people. The jungles were made up mostly of men who would hop empty railcars and steal rides from town to town. Being a hobo was a hard life, especially when railroad security guards, called bulls, would find them. Railroad bulls could be cruel, beating up hobos and throwing them off the trains.

As our train passed by the hobo jungles, I thought about how lucky we were. We were getting paying jobs that would support our families back home. Yet none of us knew what tomorrow was going to hold—or the days after that.

THREE

Camp Custer

WE ARRIVED AT CAMP CUSTER IN BATTLE CREEK IN THE EARLY afternoon. An army sergeant had us line up and called out names. When we heard "Sokolowski," Squint and I said "Here!" at the same time. He placed two checkmarks on his chart. We were then taken to a building that had medical gear, doctors, and nurses for physical examinations before we could join the CCC. The army people called the building the "infirmary."

Camp Custer was jammed to the gills with guys who were enrolling in the CCC. We stood in long lines waiting to have our teeth inspected, eyes examined, and bodies poked and prodded. Pick, Stosh, Yasku, Squint, and I stayed together, avoiding Big Mike O'Shea and his buddies. We talked nervously as we stood in the slow-moving line waiting our turn.

"What are you going to do with the money?" Squint asked, breaking the silence.

At the mention of the word money, Yasku spun around to face Squint. "What money? I didn't get no money."

"You dope," Squint said as he punched Yasku playfully on the arm, "we're gonna get paid for working in the CCC. I'm talking about the $30 we get every month. What are you gonna do with the money?"

"We don't get to keep that much," Pick laughed. "The CCC sends $25 back home each month. We get to keep $5."

"Still, that's a lot of money," I said.

"At first I was thinking that I'd buy a horse, but I changed my mind. I'm gonna save up to buy an automobile," Squint said with a chuckle. Our conversation was interrupted as the line moved forward a few steps.

"You need a lot of money to buy one of them," Stosh chimed in after a time. "And who are you going to get to drive it, Squint? You don't see good enough to drive. You'd kill somebody."

"You wait," Squint responded. A wide grin crossed his face. "I'm gonna save up a couple thousand bucks and buy a brand new LaSalle Coupe—a convertible. They make 'em in yellow. That automobile looks like sunshine rolling down the street." Squint sighed and looked around to make sure that he had everyone's attention. "When I get my LaSalle, I'll hire Jarek to do the driving."

The guys laughed and slapped Squint on the shoulder. "That was a good one, Squint," Pick said, wiping tears of laughter from his eyes. "Maybe I'll buy a LaSalle and get Yasku to drive it for me."

As we got closer and closer to the infirmary, we were split up and sent to different areas for examination. A dentist looked at my teeth first. You had to have four good teeth top and bottom to be in the CCC. You couldn't be too tall or too short. You couldn't be too skinny or weigh too much. Doctors checked us all from top to bottom—our ears, eyes, and noses.

The physical was a breeze except for the shots. I'd never been to the doctor or had a shot in my life. The needles were big and long. One of the guys ahead of me howled. Another fella fainted and they left him laying there right on the floor. We had to step over him as we approached the doctor with the needle. The doctor didn't seem to care; he just shoved and pushed the plunger, one in each arm. They felt like the hardest punches I'd ever taken.

I rubbed my arms as I left the infirmary. Outside I found Squint sitting on the steps; the few things he had brought with him that day were neatly stacked at his side. His face was streaked with tear tracks.

"Squint," I asked, "what's wrong?"

"I washed out, Jarek. They're sending me home."

I was puzzled. "What do you mean, washed out?"

Squint turned away so I couldn't see his tears. "I didn't make it. The doctor told me that my eyes are too bad for me to be in the CCC. The train back home leaves in an hour." Squint stood up and faced me as he wiped his eyes with his sleeves. I didn't know what to say. He put his arms around me and talked to me in Polish. "Now it is you who must be a man, Jarek." He sniffled quietly before continuing. "I won't be around to protect you from Mike O'Shea and others like him. Don't risk your job by fighting. Your work with the CCC is very important to our family. Promise me that you will work hard and stay out of trouble?"

The news was like a punch in the gut. I blinked away tears. There was only one word I could say—"Promise!"

FOUR

New Duds

AFTER WE ALL COMPLETED OUR PHYSICALS AND SHOTS, WE were told that we would have twenty-four hours of rest before starting our training. I wandered around aimlessly, lost in my thoughts and already missing Squint.

That afternoon, an army officer ordered us to assemble on the parade grounds, a large open area. An American flag stood tall at one end. The parade grounds were just outside of our barracks. Like everything else at Camp Custer, it was clean as a whistle. Rocks around the grounds were painted white. The lawn was cut low and well trimmed. There wasn't a loose paper or piece of trash to be seen.

We formed into neat rows and columns to take the Oath of Enrollment. My mind wandered as the words were repeated in broken chorus. "I agree to remain in the

Civilian Conservation Corps for the period of ... I will obey those in authority and observe all the rules and regulations thereof ... any articles issued to me by the United States Government for use while a member of the Civilian Conservation Corps ... I further understand that any infraction of the rules or regulations of the Civilian Conservation Corps renders me liable to expulsion therefrom. So help me God."

At Supply Headquarters, we were issued a steel cot, a cotton mattress, a pillow, two pillow cases, four sheets, mattress cover, three blankets, and a cotton comforter. They also gave each of us a mess kit. The kit contained a pot with a lid, a pan with a handle, and a cup, all contained in a nice, neat package kept in a canvas bag.

Stosh wondered aloud about the mess kit he was issued. "It don't make no sense. Everything round here is so clean, why would they want us to make a mess?"

None of us was about to argue about getting free things. So, we just took our mess kits and moved on down the line picking up more gear.

The stuff kept piling up. We were issued a canteen, four undershirts and drawers, a heavy jacket, two suits of overalls, two flannel shirts, two pairs of wool trousers, two pairs of shoes, a working hat, and a dress cap. It was like Christmas, but the gifts kept coming. We got a raincoat, overcoat, belt, necktie, six pairs of socks, working gloves, a toilet kit, towels, and a duffel bag to hold all our new gear.

The denim work clothes, shoes, and uniforms they gave us were left over from the war and were available in two sizes

... too big and too small. Pick's arms and legs stuck out of his clothes. Yasku looked like an empty sack tied in the middle. When we complained, the army supply officer just growled and told us to trade. Stosh was just happy to get new shoes, no matter what size.

Before hauling armloads of supplies to our barracks, Stosh threw his old, holey shoes in the trash. "No more hand-me-down shoes for Stoshu Campeau," he said. "I won't get no rocks between my toes no more."

Our bunks for the night were inside old green army barracks. The barracks were a collection of long rectangular buildings lined up side-by-side. Though the buildings themselves were old, they were neat and clean. Not a speck of dust was anywhere to be found, and they smelled freshly washed. Each building housed about sixty guys. Beds were placed against the sidewalls and a potbellied stove squatted in the center of each building. The olive drab woolen blankets were scratchy, but the steel cots were comfortable.

As we were getting organized, a sergeant came by the barracks and taught us how to make our beds. Some of the guys complained that they already knew how to make a bed, but the sergeant set them straight. Blankets had to be tucked perfectly and so tight that you could drop a nickel on them and it would bounce. We were expected to make our beds first thing each morning. The sergeant informed us that beds and belongings would be inspected daily. "Your mothers won't be here to pick up dirty clothes and straighten your things for you," he said. "Any questions?"

Pick shuffled his feet nervously. "Any idea of where we'll

be assigned? Do you think it'll be near Grand Rapids? It'd kinda be nice to go home from time to time."

"You won't be goin' nowhere near Grand Rapids," the sergeant said. "Most of the first enrollees are being sent to the Upper Peninsula.

"The Upper Peninsula?" someone asked. "What's it like there?"

"It's freezing cold. Winter all the time," the sergeant said in a spooky voice. "They got moose with big teeth and huge, pointy antlers. Them moose like to eat boys, ya know."

"You're kidding, right?" Yasku asked nervously.

"I am straight as a string telling you the truth," the sergeant said as he crossed his heart. "The Upper Peninsula is full of bears and wolves and mountain lions, too. Every one of 'em is hungry for fresh meat."

Stosh swallowed hard. "Bears, too?"

"That ain't the worst of it," the sergeant continued. "I heard tell that the ghost of a crazy lumberjack is wandering around the Upper Peninsula. An enlisted man from this outfit was up there and heard the story of a lumberjack who drowned in a small lake. Whenever it rains, the ghost of that lumberjack wanders around looking for people to chop up with his axe." The sergeant looked around at us. Some of the guys' eyes were as big as saucers. "His spirit rises in the rain b'cause he can't leave the water that drowned him dead."

The sergeant eyeballed the group of boys who were listening. Then he took in a deep, raspy breath. His head shook and his tongue wagged as he let out a long low howl. A few of us laughed and walked away. Several guys pestered the sergeant with questions about ghosts and beasts as he left the barracks shaking his head.

Stosh and Yasku looked a bit spooked. Pick put his arms around them and said, "Don't you guys worry. Jarek and I will protect you from man-eating moose and lumberjack ghosts."

FIVE

Swimmers and Drivers

THE FOUR OF US MANAGED TO BUNK CLOSE TO EACH OTHER. BIG
Mike and his gang were assigned to a different barrack. We
took it easy the rest of the afternoon, organizing our things
and trading clothes until we found the best fit possible. We
had new clothes, new shoes, new socks, and underwear. It
had been a long time since most of us had anything new. It
didn't matter that the stuff was left over from the war.

Later on, a soldier came by the barrack and told us to get
ready for supper. We were to report to the mess hall after we
had washed up. Mess hall? Mess halls and mess kits were
new words for us. Whatever a mess hall was, it didn't sound
like a good place to be having supper. It would take a long
time before we figured out all the different words that the
military used for things.

The mess hall was a huge, open building with rows and rows of tables. Practically everything inside and out was painted olive drab, the official color of the army. As we approached the mess hall, the smell of food made our mouths water. "I can't believe we're eating twice in the same day," Stosh said as we were paraded into the hall. "I think I might like this place."

"I hope we're having somethin' other than baked potatoes," I said. Yasku laughed.

As we took our places at a large table, we were told that there was to be no talking during dinner time in the mess hall. Tin plates and military silverware were stacked up on one end of each table. Heaping bowls of mashed potatoes, gravy, and peas were placed in front of us. Bread, butter, and pitchers of milk were at each table. Pieces of golden brown, deep-fried chicken were stacked high on platters. We dug in and ate like never before. The mess hall filled with the clatter of eating. After dinner, there was peach pie. It was heaven.

One fella at our table prayed long and hard after his meal. A wise guy sitting next to him whispered, "What you prayin' about?"

"I'm praying my family don't hear about what I had or how much food I ate tonight," the fella replied in a hushed voice.

His prayer set us all to thinking. Back home there wasn't much of anything for our families to eat. Each of us felt guilty, yet none of us could pass up the piles of food. I especially thought about Squint. I was sure that he would be going to bed hungry tonight.

As the sounds of eating slowed, a shrill whistle pierced the clatter. "Listen up," shouted the army officer we'd seen earlier. The room went silent. "My name is Lieutenant Campbell. You are going to learn a lot about military ways over the next several weeks. Let me start out by saying that the Civilian Conservation Corps isn't the army. However, when you address an officer, you are to stand at attention, eyes straight ahead, and arms sharply to your sides. Salute an officer crisply, and the officer will return your salute. You are to address officers by their rank and surname. Or, you may just refer to an officer as sir."

Lieutenant Campbell glanced around the room to make sure everyone was listening closely. "I know you've been given a twenty-four-hour rest period to recover from your shots. However, I have a few special jobs to offer, and I'm looking for volunteers."

Stosh leaned over and whispered, "I heard we shouldn't be too quick to volunteer."

Lieutenant Campbell walked back and forth at the head of the dining hall. "I need eight boys who like being around water. I prefer guys who can swim, but it isn't necessary to know how. The job is easy and you'll be given special training. If it turns out that you like beach detail, you might volunteer to do it all the time. So, do I have volunteers?"

Hands shot up across the room. Lieutenant Campbell pointed to eight eager faces. He motioned at four of them. "I want you to meet me here right after dinner. I'll take the rest of you boys to the beach tomorrow after breakfast."

I sat back in my seat thinking that maybe going to the

beach might be a good job. I regretted listening to Stosh. My thoughts were interrupted when the lieutenant spoke up again.

"Now, I need four guys who want to be truck drivers. Don't worry; you don't need to know how to drive. You will get training on the job."

Quickly I stood up to volunteer along with about half the other guys in the dining hall. Stosh tried to hold me down, but I really wanted to drive a truck. Lieutenant Campbell scanned the room, overlooking me and choosing four others. What irritated me most was that the lieutenant picked Mike O'Shea.

As the dining hall emptied and the guys headed off to their barracks, I pushed through the crowd and walked right up to the lieutenant. "Sir, I would really like to be a truck driver. I know I could do a good—"

"Next time, kid," was all he said, "next time."

"Yah, punk," Mike O'Shea said as he put his big hand on my shoulder and shoved me backward, "maybe next time." A smirk crossed his face as he sauntered out of the room.

For a moment I wanted to wipe that smile off Mike O'Shea's face right then and there. But I thought better of it. I'd promised Squint that I'd stay out of trouble.

SIX

Volunteers

AFTER SUPPER, PICK AND I WERE TALKING ON OUR BUNKS WHEN Yasku burst through the barracks door. He was doubled over in laughter. "Wait 'til you hear this," he said, gasping for breath. "Those guys who volunteered for duty on the beach ... well, they got a chance to work near the water all right. They're washing all the pots and pans and our dinner dishes. Sounds like beach duty and waterfront jobs mean doing dishes."

"See," Stosh said with a chuckle. "I told you to be careful about volunteering. My father was in the war. He told me of such things."

"I'm glad you said something," Yasku said. "The way Lieutenant Campbell described them jobs, it was mighty tempting to volunteer."

We explored Camp Custer all evening, laughing and joking about the beach workers. The camp was like a city. Aside from the barracks, mess hall, and infirmary, they had a store (called a PX), rifle ranges, training centers, and other buildings too numerous to explore. Eventually we found ourselves in one of the buildings. It had a pool table, and we played pool until they threw us out at 9:00 p.m.

Lights out was at 10:00, and everyone was expected to be in the sack and quiet at that time. Somewhere nearby our barrack, a horn played a soft, gentle tune. Later we would find out that the horn was a bugle and every night at Camp Custer the bugler played taps. As I lay in my bed listening to the music, I thought about missing my chance to be a truck driver. It still burned me that Mike O'Shea was chosen instead of me. Then I thought about Squint and the words of my father. Back home in Grand Rapids, many, many people were out of work and scratching just to stay alive. I had a job. If my father were here, he would remind me to be thankful, no matter what.

Soon the night air in the barracks was filled with the sounds of sleeping. Some of the guys snored louder than the bugler. Here and there, soft whimpers could be heard as boys experienced the loneliness of being on their own. Snores and whimpers were sounds we would all have to get used to. Though each of us was lonely, it was the first time in years that we'd gone to sleep without being hungry. In the night, someone lit a fire in the potbelly stove. Though the temperatures dropped outside, the small fire took the edge off the cold inside the barracks.

At 6:00 the next morning, the bugler played once again. This was different music than we had heard the night before. While we were at Camp Custer, the sound of reveille would wake us each morning. Arms were still sore from the shots we received the day before. Still, we got up to face the new day. Our first job was to make our beds the way we'd been shown, tight and taut. We got dressed, then picked up and organized our things. An army sergeant came around and inspected our barrack. Some boys remade their beds several times until they were "army sharp."

It was a cold day for late April. Snow and rain spit from the sky as we assembled on the parade ground. We shivered in the early morning hours. After a flag-raising ceremony, morning exercises, and breakfast, the beach workers attended to their pots and pans. The rest of us had the day off to relax. As I explored Camp Custer, I spotted Big Mike O'Shea pushing a wheelbarrow piled high with rocks. Last night's smirk was replaced with a strained grimace as he worked behind the heavy wheelbarrow.

This was the first time I really took a good look at Mike O'Shea. He was three or four inches taller than me, maybe six feet, with broad shoulders and long thick arms. His head was square like a cinder block. He wore his carrot-orange hair cut close. Freckles dotted his face. The thing that caught my attention was the hard look he had in his eyes and the scowl he wore on his face. If his prediction that he and I would have it out one day was correct, he would be a handful. Still, I was less afraid of him than I was of losing the job that would keep my family alive.

As I watched him push the heavy wheelbarrow around, I understood what it meant to volunteer to be a truck driver. In the army, as in the Civilian Conservation Corps, driving a truck and pushing a wheelbarrow were often one and the same. It was just like a beach worker was a dishwasher. We learned quickly that our army leaders would twist words to make volunteering for extra work sound like fun.

Mike had worked up a good sweat driving his truck in the cool morning air. He grunted with strain as he pushed his load. Despite my promise to Squint that I would steer clear of trouble, I couldn't resist poking fun at him. "Look," I said laughing and pointing at Mike O'Shea and his one-wheeled truck. "Is that truck a Ford or a Chevrolet?"

The army enlisted man who was supervising the work glared at me. "Unless you want to join your friend, you'll keep your mouth shut."

Big Mike wiped the sweat from his brow and spit. "He ain't no friend of mine."

SEVEN

Training

THE NEXT THREE WEEKS WERE CONSUMED BY DAILY EXERCISES, classes, and job training. The military had all of us CCC boys going from sun-up to sun-down and later. We were all fingerprinted and issued serial numbers. The disk on the chain around my neck read: CC6-104377.

Though there was little time for anything else, my brother was on my mind every day and night. I worried about him. To be honest, I also worried about myself. Squint was older and bigger than me. He had always been my hero and protector—the only person I could turn to in good times and bad. I counted on him as he did me. We had been a team ever since we were little. Now the team was separated. Growing up would be harder without him.

Big Mike was a constant problem. He was a cloud of trouble that seemed to follow me around Camp Custer, no matter where I went. He continued to go out of his way each day to make life a little more miserable for me and my friends. I wasn't all that concerned about him pushing me around. I could take care of myself. I was more worried about holding down my temper and keeping my job in the CCC. The military officers made it clear that they didn't want any trouble. Fighting could be used as grounds for dismissal. I vowed to keep my promise to Squint: to keep my job and keep my nose clean. That promise would prove to be a hard one to keep.

Morning seemed to come earlier and earlier each day at Custer. Most of us had never experienced formal exercises like sit-ups, push-ups, chin-ups, jumping jacks, and stretching exercises. We'd spent some time running around the neighborhood back home, but never two miles or more at a stretch. Our leaders told us we'd have to be in good shape for the work ahead.

Most days, after breakfast, army sergeants gave us work training. We learned how to sharpen and handle axes, picks, crosscut saws, and shovels. They taught us how to use tools we'd never seen or heard of before: mattocks, fire rakes, and grub hoes. Then we were split into teams and given jobs that put those tools to work.

Pick, Yasku, and I were on a team with several other guys. Stosh was assigned to a group of boys from Detroit. Yasku was the first on our team to volunteer to demonstrate how to use an axe. At one time, he'd helped his father split and deliver wood to earn money. As he stepped up to the tree, he bragged about his skills as a woodsman.

We stood back as Yasku put all he had into his first swing. The axe head struck at an angle. Rather than taking a bite into the wood, the sharp blade made a ringing sound as it glanced off the tree trunk. The handle twisted, and Yasku lost his grip. The axe flew end-over-end, and headed straight for a group of guys who were horsing around. At the last possible moment they saw it coming. The handle struck one fella in the knee with a loud *tha-wack*! Another guy jumped straight up in the air as the blade swept beneath his legs before skidding harmlessly across the ground.

The sergeant who was supervising the training went into a rage. Yasku hung his head as the sergeant ranted. The guys who had nearly been struck stared him down as the sergeant tore into them for not paying attention. Tool training was cancelled for the rest of the week. Instead, we took classes in safety and first aid. Somehow, though, we managed to survive tool training with a few cuts and bruises, but no broken bones, lost fingers, or toes.

Another part of our training involved setting up, taking down, and folding tents. We first practiced on what were called umbrella tents. No one needed to explain why they were called umbrellas. When they were set up right, they took on the appearance of an umbrella that was about half open. Like almost all the gear and equipment in the CCC, they were army leftovers. Once we were sent to our permanent camp, we would live in tents until barracks could be constructed.

The first task in setting up the tent was to unfold it and lay the canvas flat on the ground. My job was to raise the center pole. The old canvas was heavy and stunk of mold and mildew. I crawled underneath, feeling for the hole that would be the resting place for the center pole. Once I inserted the pole, I raised the tent as far as I could; then my job was to hold it in place. When the tent pole stood tall and proud, lines would be pegged into the ground to give the tent its shape and stability.

Umbrella tents were fairly easy to put up. Once we could handle them, we moved on to the larger tents that would be required for our camp. Mess tents were like circus tents. The size and weight of the canvas of these tents were hard to believe. Setting up the bigger tents required teamwork and muscle. Umbrella tents were secured with stakes or pegs that could be driven into the ground with single–bladed axes or hammers. For mess tents, ten–pound sledge hammers were used to drive the huge stakes down into the earth.

In the afternoons and evenings at Camp Custer we took classes in fire fighting, construction, road building, and stringing telephone lines. We learned that the CCC would be stringing phone lines so that wildfires could be reported back to our base camp from remote areas. Back home only one of the neighbors on our entire block had a telephone. Now we were going to put up telephone lines in the wilderness.

Some guys decided that they wanted to be cooks and bakers. Camp Custer offered cooking classes for them. Some CCC enrollees learned how to operate heavy equipment like bulldozers and tractors. Others were trained for office jobs. They took typing classes and learned how to manage an office.

The days flew by. We hit the sack each night tired and

sore. The combination of hard work and good food made changes in us. The skinny cats were putting muscle and meat on their bones.

Just like the sergeant told us on our first day at Camp Custer, a rumor went around that our work assignment would take us to the far north. That information meant little to us city boys—other than the lingering doubts about the monsters and ghosts prowling that area. When you've never been more than a few blocks from home, the Upper Peninsula of Michigan might just as well be the moon.

Little did we know that we would be heading for a place that looked like no place we'd ever seen. We were headed for the wilderness.

EIGHT

North Bound
May 1934

WE LEFT FOR THE UPPER PENINSULA ONCE OUR TRAINING WAS
completed. We boarded a train that took us from Battle
Creek to Kalamazoo. There we transferred to the Northland
Express train that would take us up to Mackinaw City. The
guys and I sat in seats as far away from Mike O'Shea as we
could. As we chatted with those around us, we learned that
some of the other fellas had their fill of Mike and his pushy
ways. As the train rolled north, we made friends and swapped
stories of home.

The train screeched to a stop at the station in Grand
Rapids. Though the station wasn't more than a few blocks
from home, we weren't allowed to get off the train. It would
have been nice to say goodbye one more time and to check
up on Squint to make sure he was all right. In Grand Rapids,

we took on more passengers before striking out for Comstock Park, Howard City, Big Rapids, and parts north. Stosh and Yasku were snoring like lumberjacks while Pick and I played a few hands of cards as the train bumped along the rough tracks.

Between hands, I studied Yasku as he slept. His mouth hung open as he snored and slobbered on himself. He wore his hair cut short. His thin, hollow cheeks made his long nose seem even longer.

None of us had had easy lives. Yasku's was worst of all. His father died a few years after he returned from the war. The mustard gas that eventually took him was a terrible weapon. Then, when Yasku's mother passed, he was left to raise his brothers and sisters. Though he had help from an aunt who lived nearby, Yasku was the man of the house. He left school after the fifth grade to take a job in a foundry in downtown Grand Rapids. Yasku couldn't read or write very well, but none of us ever mentioned it in conversation. We all pitched in to help him with letters to and from home.

As the train rocked over the rails, Yasku bounced around in his seat. I couldn't help but smile. He wasn't the smartest fellow I'd ever met, but, he had a big heart. Yasku was the kind of friend that could make you smile, no matter what.

Small towns, deserted farms, and rough countryside passed outside our passenger car. Wherever the rails took us, we saw just how the Depression had taken hold. Much of the farmland that once grew corn, wheat, and soybeans had been repossessed by the banks. Now weeds and tall brush were taking over the once-bountiful farms. Fence lines were broken down. Farmhouses and barns once full of energy and activity were now empty and without life.

The thick pine forests of the north we had heard about as school children were nowhere to be found. Instead, we saw reduced to mile after mile of ugly stumps and scrub brush. Tree limbs from cut timber were left in drying piles on the ground. During our orientation, we were told that our job would be to help conserve our forests and state. To my view, there wasn't much left to be saved.

The view outside the window didn't change much as we rolled north. Occasionally we would see families walking alongside the tracks. Children followed their parents quietly. Sometimes babies were carted along in wobbly wagons. Sad looks on tired faces told the whole story. Work was hard, if not impossible, to find. People were hungry. Many were broken down just like the farmhouses alongside the tracks. It was hurtful to look out the window. It was easier just to close my eyes.

I heard the screeching sounds just before feeling the shock of the brakes. When the train's brakes grabbed, CCC boys and duffle bags went flying forward, rolling toward the engine as its wheels dug into the tracks. Train cars racked against each other as the locomotive ground to a halt. Yasku smacked into the seat next to me and split his lip. Blood was everywhere. After the long screeching halt, Lieutenant Campbell rushed through the car. "Everybody out," he said. "Help get the cows off the tracks. And, watch out for cow pies."

Cows? Cow pies?

"Wow," Pick said. "The closest I've ever been to a real cow was a piece of bacon."

Stosh screwed up his face and said, "Bacon don't come from cows. It comes from pigs."

"Well," Pick said, "pigs live by cows, don't they? You know, they live by cows in barns."

Even Yasku laughed, his upper teeth outlined in the red of blood. "Oww-w," he said, holding his mouth. "It hurts to laugh." I handed him a clean handkerchief and he pressed it to his split lip.

We climbed down out of the train car and headed in the direction of the locomotive. None of us had a clue as to what a cow pie was, but we didn't want to ask anyone about it. The engine hissed as clouds of steam escaped from its boiler. Up ahead the engineer blew the whistle and rang the bell. Before long we were at the head of the train, standing by a herd of big, smelly cows.

We were amazed at their size. Their thick, white hides were splotched with large black spots. Coarse hairs covered their bodies and long tails with a swatch of hair on the end swished back and forth. The cows mooed gently, but they stubbornly held their positions. Stosh, Pick, and I pushed at the backside of one of them, keeping away from strong back legs. Yasku tried talking to it.

"Come on, cow," Yasku said in Polish. "You ain't safe here on the railroad tracks. Go home, cow, go home." That didn't work. So he tried something else. "Do you want some nice cheese?" Yasku asked, pretending to hold some cheese in front of the cow's nose.

Pick, Stosh, and I laughed so hard that we fell away from the cow and held our sides. "Cows don't eat cheese, you knucklehead," I said. "Cheese is made from cows' milk."

"Really?" Yasku asked. His fat lip made the word sound funny.

His response was so serious and so stupid, we fell to our knees in laughter. Strangely enough, the cow started walking off. "Maybe cows understand Polish," Yasku said through his fat lip.

"Sure," Pick said, "and maybe she likes cheese."

By the time the animal had cleared the tracks, it was heading downhill at a brisk pace. Here and there, other groups of CCC boys were making slow progress with the cows.

As we worked on another, we heard a burst of laughter from behind us. Mike O'Shea stood at the center of a circle of guys. In his hand he held a long, thick branch. O'Shea took the club and beat the backside of a cow with it. The poor animal reared up and trotted off, bawling as it ran. The cow's reaction caused another burst of laughter.

"What a jerk," I said.

Pick took me by the shoulder and turned me away from Big Mike. "Pay no attention."

Other guys took to using clubs on the cows. Before long, the tracks were cleared, and we were back aboard. As the Northland Express continued climbing to the top of the Lower Peninsula of Michigan, guys shared cow stories. One of the fellas in our train car discovered what a cow pie was when he slipped and fell into one. Though he changed his clothes, the foul smell stayed with us the rest of the trip. Everybody had a good laugh over the cow pie. Still, I was sickened by Mike O'Shea's cruelty. There was no need for him to beat on those cows.

He and I would have it out some day.

NINE

Beyond the Waters

May 1934

WE WERE WEARY AND RESTLESS BY THE TIME THE TRAIN pulled in to Mackinaw City late in the day. The blue water ahead was a beautiful sight. Waves crashed ashore as gulls swooped and soared in the sky above us. As we stepped out of the railroad car and onto the train platform, we shuddered in the cold breeze that came off the big water. We were issued vouchers that could be used to buy supper, then we were free to explore Mackinaw City until lights out.

Stosh and I took a walk down to the docks to see the ferry boats and to look out at the sliver of land across the distance of water, the Upper Peninsula. We headed back to the hotel as the sun went down across the Straits and the evening temperature dropped. Fishing boats moored offshore bobbed in the rough water. Even the large ferries rolled in the waves.

The night was spent in a cheap hotel in town, six boys in a room. In the morning, our railroad cars would be switched over to another line and transported across the lake on a huge boat called a railroad ferry. Near the docks, railroad tracks formed a spider web of main lines, crossings, and sidings. The tracks would feed railcars into and out of the gaping mouths of the car ferries.

Before lights-out, there were rumors going around about railroad car ferries and the dark waters that separated the two peninsulas of Michigan. In the lobby of our hotel, an old-timer was spinning tales about the lakes and those who crossed them. He wore the checkered flannels of a woodsman. From what I could see, he had just a few teeth in his mouth. While he talked, he chewed on the stem of an old corncob pipe.

He told the story of the S.S. *Milwaukee*, a car ferry that went to the bottom of Lake Michigan with all hands on board in October of '29. "When the lake got rough, the boat tossed stem to stern," he remembered. "The railcars deep inside the steel hull broke free. They rattled around loose in the hold, smashing and crashing."

The old-timer paused and looked around at the wide eyes staring back at him. Most of the CCC boys were scared stiff. He knocked gray ash from his pipe. "With no warning, the boat capsized and slipped beneath the cold, cold waves. They didn't have a chance, them boys on the *Milwaukee*. Bodies and life jackets from the railroad car ferry washed up on Michigan beaches for miles around. To this very day," the old-timer concluded, "you can hear them poor souls calling in the wind on nights like tonight."

A howling gust came off the lake. The wind shook the shutters and banged at the windows of the old hotel. Pick nearly jumped out of his skin with fright.

We all hit the sack that night with unsettled thoughts. First it was the sergeant's tall tales back at Camp Custer; now this old-timer was getting us all worked up.

Early the next morning, we nervously climbed aboard our train. A locomotive then pushed our railcars onto the ferry. The railroad car ferry was a 339-foot-long steel ship that had four sets of railroad tracks inside. We were told that the ship could hold twenty-two fully loaded railcars. The sole purpose of the *Chief Wawatam* was to transport passengers and railroad cars back and forth across the Straits of Mackinac. Railcars were loaded from the front, or bow, of the ship.

We were given the choice of staying in our seats on the train or going up on deck to watch the trip topside. I decided to stay put on the train. As the railcar bumped and jerked its way onto the ship, I caught a quick glimpse of the lake. Maybe it was my imagination, but the waves looked taller and more menacing than they had the day before. We all looked straight ahead as the dim light of the ship's interior wrapped around us. As the *Chief Wawatam* continued to be loaded with people and railroad cars, the old-timer's story of the S.S. *Milwaukee* was on my mind. The car went quiet.

"This is like that story the nuns at St. Adalbert's told us," Stosh said nervously, trying to break the silence. "Remember Jonah and the whale?"

"Sure, I remember that one," Pick said. "This swallowing

part ain't too bad ... I only hope we get spit out like we're supposed to."

The *Chief Wawatam* creaked and groaned as she left the dock in Mackinaw City. Her large propellers took big chomping bites of water and moved the ship steadily forward. The wind and waves pushed at the ship, causing it to rise and fall, roll and pitch. Some of the guys got real sick.

After what seemed like hours on the ship, we felt a sudden bump that was accompanied by the crash of metal striking something solid. We sat up stock straight as a loud whining sound came from the ship. Yasku's eyes were wide with fear. Before panic swept through the train, someone shouted that we had docked at St. Ignace. After a time, the railroad car lurched again and we were pulled out of the *Chief Wawatam*. We were spit out into the daylight, just like the story of Jonah and the whale.

The railroad line followed a trail out of St. Ignace through the wilderness of Michigan's Upper Peninsula. The tracks were in rough shape after a severe winter in the north.

Rocks, swamps, and barren land passed as we rolled on through the morning hours. Miles of tree stumps and piles of dried brush littered the countryside. The train bounced along rough tracks for hours and hours. As we headed west through the Upper Peninsula, rain pelted the train. It came down in sheets with lightning crashing around us.

The train rolled to a noisy stop at an abandoned railroad siding. We saw no town, no buildings, just miles and miles of nothing. We were ordered to unload our supplies. When the train left the siding, we stood there in the rain among piles of food, tents, bedding, cooking gear, and tools.

We were told that our home was called Camp Polack
Lake. Mike and a few of his friends were sure to make fun
of the Polish-sounding name.

TEN

Polack Lake

WE CARRIED SUPPLIES TO A CAMPSITE THAT WAS A HALF MILE
away from the train tracks. After a time, a few forestry trucks
arrived to haul the heavy stuff. We made several trips along
the muddy road, lugging duffle bags and supplies. Stosh and
Yasku kept a close eye out for man-eating moose and the
lumberjack ghost. Polack Lake wasn't far from our campsite.
The water was gray, cold, and shallow. It wasn't the beautiful
swimming hole that Pick imagined it to be.

The cooks began to assemble a makeshift kitchen as
we hauled load after load. Fires were lit and pots of water
were put on to heat. The area surrounding us was both
awesome and frightening. It was like nothing we'd seen
before—nothing we could ever have imagined. Tree stumps
dotted the countryside in every direction for as far as we

could see. Branches that once carried emerald green pine needles now lay scattered along the ground, brown and dead. In some areas, dead branches were piled waist high. The ground itself was rutted and scarred by the thousands of tree trunks that had been cut off at the base then dragged off to the lumber mill.

Everything was colored dull brown or gray. Even the sky itself was a dreadful gray. The rain was cold. The ground was still frozen hard as a rock in areas. Fingers of snow reached out from the shadows. Ice hung at the fringes of standing water that gathered in the low areas. It was like winter was trying to keep its cold grip on the land. The only color to be seen was the dull olive drab of the army equipment and clothing we wore.

There were no sounds of motors or engines. There were no foundry noises, city noises, or people noises. Nothing but the constant tap of rain. Even the flocks and formations of birds that were moving north in their spring migrations were quieted in their travels.

"Holy smokes," Stosh said, his body shivering with cold. "What have we gotten ourselves into here?"

As we looked around and took in the view, the air began to fill with the smells of food cooking. Our attention shifted from our surroundings to the thought of lunch. Soon two hundred hungry CCC boys were circling around the cooks. Each held a mess kit open and ready to be filled.

"Listen up," the lieutenant called. We all snapped to attention. "You're a long way from home. By my reckoning, we're about five miles from nowhere. It will take us several days to get this camp together, and we've got a lot of work to do before we can bed down for the night. So, let me introduce you to your camp commander."

The camp commander's voice boomed through the cool air. "At ease, gentlemen," Captain Mason said. We relaxed our posture as the captain continued. "Lieutenant Campbell is correct; we are in the middle of nowhere."

He pointed to the east. "If you don't like the work, or if you want to run home to mama, St. Ignace is a four- or five-day walk in that direction. You can try to hop a train, but they don't stop to pick up passengers here. You'd have to jump on board while it's rolling full speed." Then the camp commander pointed to the southeast, "Manistique is about forty miles that way, give or take. You might be able to catch a boat to the Lower Peninsula there. However, if you choose to go 'over the hill,' I'd recommend that you pack food and water.

"Now," the camp commander continued, "if you choose to stay, you will be a part of something very important, something that will last for generations. Together, we're going to turn nowhere into somewhere. It will take time, and it will take work—lots of it. Over the next few days, we're going to concentrate on building our camp. Over the next six months, we're going to begin transforming our camp and the surrounding countryside.

"We're going to break out the tools and clear the area right after lunch is over. Once we've prepared the campsite, we'll have to set up tents and beds in an orderly fashion before we hit the sack. Leaders have been chosen to direct the work. The sooner you get your jobs done, the sooner you can catch some shut-eye."

The captain let his message sink in before continuing. "This is the Civilian Conservation Corps, gentlemen. We are not wet nurses or babysitters. Remember the Oath of Enrollment you took. You are to obey the orders of those who have been put in charge. Furthermore, you are expected to follow the chain of command at all times. If you've got a question, a problem, or a bellyache, take it to your assistant leader—not to Lieutenant Campbell and not to me. Is that understood?"

Silence hung in the air. "Get your fill of lunch because it will be a long time 'til supper. One final thing: Anybody who doesn't work will face KP. Dismissed!"

For lunch we had stew and corn bread. Assistant leaders then organized us into work crews. From the back of a truck, shovels, axes, and grub hoes were handed out, and we headed off in separate directions to tackle the work.

Of all the rotten luck, our assistant leader was none other than Big Mike O'Shea.

ELEVEN

Something from Nothing

BIG MIKE DELIGHTED IN SHOWING OFF HIS NEWFOUND authority as an assistant leader. The harder we worked, the more he pushed. Mike gave the dirtiest and hardest jobs to me and my buddies. We cut brush and moved thorny branches all afternoon and into the night. After dark, we worked in the light from supply trucks and a bonfire that was tended by one of the enrollees.

The rain stung, the wind howled, and the temperature dropped. Now and then we could see that flakes of snow were mixed in with the rain. Despite the army rain ponchos we wore, all of us were shaking with cold and soaked to the bone.

While Yasku and I were hauling branches and brush to a pile outside the campsite, a hot ember drifted down and landed in a dry bed of pine needles that was sheltered from the rain. Though the brush pile was soaking wet, the burning pine needles started the pile afire. Flames grew as they were fanned by the wind.

I looked around and spotted a finger of snow nearby. I grabbed handfuls of the grainy snow and threw it on the flames. The fire hissed at me like a snake. Yasku started taking the pile apart, kicking at branches. We worked feverishly. When Yasku and I returned to the work crew, our hands were burned, and we were blackened by ash and soot.

"Where have you goldbricks been?" Mike snarled as he spotted us.

Yasku and I looked at each other. He spoke first as he pointed back at the brush pile. "We was just back there helpin' out ..."

Mike stepped forward. His eyes glowed in the dim light. "I don't want excuses. I expect you to work."

"We're not making excuses," I said. "We were putting out a fire."

Mike grabbed me by the shirt. "Your job is to haul brush and wood, not put out fires. You two are on KP tomorrow. If I catch you goofing off again, you'll be on KP for a week."

It was clear that Mike wasn't going to listen to our side of the argument, so we accepted our fate and went quietly back to work. In the night, hands were blistered by rough axe handles and cut by the thorns and heavy underbrush. A first-aid station was set up sometime in the evening, and it was kept hopping busy. An army medic and some volunteers worked through the night patching up wounded workers.

Though he was cruel, Mike and his work crew accomplished more than any of the other teams. That caught the attention of the lieutenant. "Keep up the good work, O'Shea," the lieutenant said. Big Mike seemed to relish the praise he was given.

The rough campsite was cleared, and umbrella tents were pitched before midnight. I shared a tent with Stosh, Yasku, Pick, and two other guys. We didn't take the time to introduce ourselves. The canvas was soaked and had a moldy, musty smell. The legs of our cots were on rough, uneven ground and wobbled whenever we rolled around. We didn't care. We slept in our wet clothes, too tired to eat, wash, or change.

At 4:00 a.m., while the others slept, Yasku and I were shaken awake by rough hands. It was Mike O'Shea. "Rise and shine, you goldbricks. Everybody who worked last night gets to sleep in today. You get to pull KP."

Stosh and I were to find out that KP, or Kitchen Police, was punishment, pure and simple. It was work upon work. After digging stumps, hauling brush, and setting up tents through the night, Yasku and I spent the early hours of the day peeling potatoes, scrubbing pots and pans, and cutting firewood for the cook stoves.

After breakfast, Yasku and I joined the rest of our work crew. Both of us worked hard in order to avoid any more KP. Setting up the mess tent and other large buildings was the order of the day. High winds that swept the area made the job difficult. Doing KP before starting work for the day made the job seem impossible. After a long day, I collapsed on my cot.

Later that evening, rain tapped against the roof of the

mess tent as we sat down to supper. The cooks made chipped beef on toast. The toast was burned and tasted like shingles, but we didn't complain. After our meal, Lieutenant Campbell told us that we would start our real jobs in the next few days. A forestry agent from the U.S. Department of Agriculture was due to show up to talk about the work ahead. With Mike in control, I saw only agony and trouble in the future. Still there was little I could do; my family was counting on me and me alone.

Gradually, the camp took shape. Like Captain Mason said, we were creating something out of nothing. Our official designation was Company 688, Camp Polack Lake.

TWELVE

The Pit

CAMP POLACK LAKE WAS NOTHING LIKE CAMP CUSTER. THERE were no buildings with windows, only tents that let in the wind and the rain. We didn't even have the luxury of a bugler to give us a tune each morning and night. Instead, we had a whistle. The morning whistle blew at 6:00 a.m. We made our beds and cleaned up inside the close quarters of our tent. Teeth chattered in the early morning air as we struggled to get into cold clothes. Then it was formation for morning exercises. Before breakfast, like all the days that were to follow at Polack Lake, we lined up and policed the site, picking up trash and debris. We also endured daily inspections. After a flag-raising ceremony, it was off to breakfast.

The pancakes were heavenly. Stosh, Pick, Yasku, and I sat together with the other fellows from our tent. Pick ate like there was no tomorrow. Even though he was over six feet tall, he only weighed about 125 pounds. The blend of melted butter and syrup made eating the hotcakes like dessert. With full bellies, we were herded out onto the parade grounds at the center of our campsite to report for duty.

Lieutenant Campbell introduced us to the forester. Mister Wilson bit off a piece of plug chewing tobacco. He spoke with the chaw in his mouth, stopping occasionally to spit a smear of brown liquid.

"Look around, gentlemen," Mr. Wilson said. "This land was once covered with beautiful pine trees. Some were 100 feet tall, maybe more. 'Bout forty years ago, almost all of that timber was harvested. The lumber crews cut the trees and slashed off the branches. They hauled off the trunks and the slashings were left behind. The lumber barons made a lot of money in their time, but they left us a big, ugly mess."

He continued, "They darn near took all the pine. Now this area is covered with stumps, brush, and trees that the lumber barons didn't want." Mr. Wilson gestured to the countryside just outside our camp. "Our job will be to clear the area and build roads to prevent wildfires. Who knows? We may be called on to fight fires as well. Come next year, we'll be planting trees in this area."

Mr. Wilson went on to tell us that the limbs and tree branches that were stacked into slashing piles across the state created serious fire hazards. Our first task as the CCC was to do all we could to reduce wildfires. He called the job "pre-suppression." That meant building roads and fire trails, constructing watchtowers, and stringing telephone lines that would link the towers to the camp. If and when the time came, we would put our lives on the line fighting fires in the wilderness.

"Fellas," Lieutenant Campbell concluded, "your assistant leaders will be assigning you to teams and passing out jobs based on your skills. Remember what Captain Mason said earlier: This is the Civilian Conservation Corps. We ain't your mommies. Work hard and keep your noses clean. I don't want no trouble from any of you. If you have problems or questions, take them to your assistant leaders."

My heart sank as Mike O'Shea approached. "I've got a special job for you boys." He glared directly at me. "You'll be in charge of supplying road construction materials. It's up to you to make sure that the road crews get the gravel they need."

Road construction materials—sounded good; maybe I'd even have a chance to drive a truck. After all, workers and materials had to be delivered to areas where roads were being built. Optimism faded away when we were handed shovels and marched to a gravel pit that was a few miles from camp. There we began our work.

Drivers backed huge dump trucks into the gravel pit. Once they parked, Stosh, Pick, Yasku, and I loaded each truck by hand—shovelful by shovelful. Ice-cold water seeped through the gravel. In short order, our feet were soaked and miserable. That was the least of it. Hour after hour we picked up the gravel and tossed it far overhead into the trucks. It was backbreaking work. At lunchtime, we sat at the edge of the pit and ate our sandwiches. Our arms were so sore and tired the sandwiches seemed heavy.

Work in the gravel pit went on day after day, five days a week. The days lasted forever, and the nights were a blink. One day Pick took me aside. "Mike is always going to keep us in this pit or someplace worse. Why don't you try to clear things up? Maybe we'd have a chance for something a little easier."

What Pick said made sense. After supper, I tracked Mike down to talk things through. My hand reached out to him. "I think we got off on a bad foot," I began. "I just want you to know that I don't have any hard feelings."

"Well, I do have hard feelings." Mike poked his finger into my chest to punctuate his words. "If you're here to get buddy-buddy with me, I don't want it."

I stepped back and looked him in the eye. "What do you want?" I asked.

"I want you and your pals to pay for making me look like a fool."

A big-mouthed response was on the tip of my tongue, but I didn't say it. Mike didn't need anyone else to make a fool out of him. He was good at making a fool of himself by the way he acted. Talking to Mike O'Shea was impossible.

THIRTEEN

Pain from the Sky

WE IGNORED MIKE O'SHEA AND THE CONSTANT TAUNTS HE delivered both at camp and in the pit. Our work continued regardless of the weather. In fact, we were told that the only time we wouldn't be outside working was if the temperature was lower than twenty degrees below zero. The month of May had been cold and rainy so far, but not that cold. The weather took a change for the better one day, or so we thought.

Down in the gravel pit, we couldn't always tell which way the wind was blowing. Early on that particular day, we felt a breeze on our backs for the first time since our jobs began. The wind had shifted and was coming out of the south. The air carried warmer temperatures and the first smells of spring.

Before long, our shirts were off and we were feeling

charged up at the promise of warmer weather yet to come. That morning seemed to fly by. We were all surprised and pleased to see the lunch truck roll up to the pit. The driver laid on the horn to tell us to come and get it.

As we sprinted up to the lunch truck, the driver poked his head out the window. "Looks like there's a storm coming up from the south. D'ya needs me to grab some rain ponchos and run 'em back to ya?"

Mike O'Shea appeared out of nowhere. It seemed as though he was always showing up at the wrong time. "Don't bother trying to help these guys. They don't have the sense to get in out of the rain. Heck, they're so stupid they won't know it's raining unless somebody tells 'em."

Mike slapped his knee as he laughed. The driver stared at him and shook his head. I just wrote off the whole situation as another example of how Mike made himself look foolish. I wasn't going to let O'Shea spoil this first nice day since coming to Polack Lake.

"You guys quit lollygagging," Mike said as we enjoyed our lunches. "Some of the drivers and road crews are complaining that you ain't keeping up with your share of the work."

We all knew better than to believe what Mike was saying. The drivers were always telling us that we were working hard and doing a good job in a bad situation. They also told us that the road crews were working hard and could barely keep up with the gravel we were sending to them. Still, none of us was about to argue with Mike. When he realized that he wasn't going to get us riled up, he stomped off to check up on other work crews.

I turned to the lunch truck driver. "Don't pay any attention to Mike," I said. "He's got a mean streak in him."

"You fellas are good workers. I'd be happy to bring back some ponchos if you want," he said.

"No thanks," I said. "I think we'll be fine. A little spring rain might even feel good."

"Yah," Pick added. "It's starting to get right warm down in that pit."

"Well, be sure to take shelter if we get lightning." With that, the driver waved and headed out to complete his deliveries to the other work crews.

We watched the storm coming as our lunches settled. "I don't like the look of them clouds," Yasku said.

"Me neither," said Stosh.

"Where would we go if the lightning starts crashing around us?" asked Pick.

"The pit is probably as good a place as any," Yasku said. "Don't lightning usually strike high points like trees and flag poles?"

"There's too much water in the pit," I said. "If lightning strikes a river or lake nearby, we could get electrocuted."

Pick came up with a solution. "We could crawl under a gravel truck. That would get us out of the rain and protect us from lightning."

We all agreed to the plan.

The storm got closer and closer through the afternoon. The sky was taken over by tall, black clouds that roiled and boiled. Just as we finished loading a truck with gravel, the warm south wind seemed to stop all of a sudden. We watched the truck roll away and were waiting for the next one to arrive when the storm hit.

The dark sky covered us. Day became night. A sudden wind from the north turned our skin prickly and the air carried a frightful cold. We heard it long before we saw or felt it. A roaring sound started off in the distance and approached us rapidly. Our plan to hide under a gravel truck had gone bad. There were no trucks around and no shelter in sight. We were caught out in the open.

Hailstones smashed to the ground all around. They were bigger around than our thumbs and struck with the force of a thrown rock. I covered my head with the blade of my shovel. The other guys did the same. The stones pinged off the shovels that protected our heads. Our arms, backs, and legs took the brunt of the stones as they fell from high above.

The hailstorm lasted only a few minutes, but it seemed like it went on for hours. Just before it let up, another gravel truck arrived and backed down into the pit to take on another load. Like the storm was on some kind of switch, the hail stopped when the truck driver turned off the engine and set the parking break. Our shelter from the storm had arrived too late to offer any help at all.

The driver stepped out of his truck and wiped his brow with his cap. "Whew, that was quite a hailstorm wasn't it?"

"Really?" Stosh asked. "We hadn't noticed."

Our mouths hung open as we looked at the truck driver. Each of us was bruised and bloody from being left out in the open without shelter. As the driver turned his back on us to walk to the rim of the pit, we grabbed handfuls of hailstones and pitched them at him.

That was to be one of the most miserable days we were to spend at Camp Polack Lake. The hailstorm had leveled our camp. Many tents were knocked down and blown away. The mess tent was ripped to shreds. The trucks were dinged and dented, windshields smashed and shattered. The storm destroyed practically everything we'd built over the past few weeks. After a day of working in the pit and being caught in an awful hailstorm, we had to begin the work of rebuilding our camp.

It took nearly a week to patch tents and fix all the damage. We did all the repairs in the evening after a long day's work.

FOURTEEN

Attack
June 1934

MIKE O'SHEA HAD WORK RESPONSIBILITIES THAT TOOK HIM to different projects in the area, so we never knew when he'd show up at the pit. We kept our backs to the work even when Mike was nowhere to be found. During our lunch break one day, the drivers left their gravel trucks and took a walk. Pick was off exploring when he spotted something in the brush nearby.

"Hey, look!" he shouted.

Pick began chasing something through the underbrush. He zigged and zagged through the nearby thicket. Now and then we'd catch a glimpse of him and the critter he was chasing. The dark animal squealed as it charged up the backside of a nearby oak tree. Pick wasn't far behind. As he climbed, the animal scurried higher and started to bleat. We didn't know whether the animal was friendly or not, so we grabbed our shovels and joined the chase.

"What is it?" Yasku shouted up at Pick.

"Don't know," Pick hollered back. "Maybe it's a dog."

"You rube," Stosh laughed, "dogs don't climb trees. Maybe it's some kind of wildcat."

The answer came quickly. Mother bear crossed the nearby clearing like a black landslide. She took up a position at the base of the tree, tilted her head back, and clacked her teeth. All of us on the ground backed away nervously. The bear issued a sound like a long, low train whistle. Our hair stood on end. Stosh jumped behind a tall stump and peeked out occasionally.

"Oh no! Oh no! Oh no!" Pick repeated as he feverishly searched for an escape. His eyes moved left and right, up and down, desperately looking for some way, any way, to save himself from an angry bear.

"Get out of there!" Yasku hollered up to Pick.

"I can't!" Pick screamed in terror. "Help me!"

The black bear circled the oak, then began to climb. She hung just below Pick. Her head swung back and forth as she continued to make loud clacking sounds with her teeth. Pick was trapped between mother and her baby. The cub clung to the only branch nearby that would hold Pick's weight. Mother inched her way up, peeling bark from the tree with her sharp claws.

"We've got to do something," I said to the guys. "If Pick gets out of there alive, we'll have to keep the bear away from him. Be ready with your shovels and follow me."

"Help!" Pick screamed desperately.

Stosh threw a rock at the mother bear, striking her in the back with a dull thud. It had no effect whatsoever. The bear inched upward and took a swipe at Pick.

"Climb, Pick! The cub is sitting on a strong branch—climb up to it, then swing out and away from the bear," I shouted.

"Are you crazy?" Pick screamed. "I don't want to get anywhere near that bear baby! Its ma will tear me to pieces!"

I hollered back, "When you climb further up the tree, the cub will go higher."

Eyes wide with fear, Pick pulled himself up slowly. When the cub scooted farther up the tree trunk, Pick swung his body out on the branch. His feet were just above the mother. "Good bear. Good bear. Pay no attention to me. Just get your baby," Pick pleaded.

Hand-over-hand, he moved farther and farther away from the tree trunk. The cub cried and the mother bear continued to clack her teeth loudly. We edged toward the tree, holding our tools up, ready to strike in Pick's defense.

The branch bent under Pick's weight. When he was out about six feet from the trunk of the tree, mother bear scampered up to reach her cub. With her baby protected, once again she took a swipe at Pick, her claws falling short of their mark. Coming so close, the claws caused Pick to lose his grip on the branch, and he tumbled out of the tree. He grunted as he took several limbs with him on the way down before falling hard on the ground.

"What's going on here?" shouted one of the truck drivers from behind us.

"Is that a bear?" asked the other.

Just then, mother and cub scuttled down the tree and hurried off into the woods. When she was off a fair distance, the bear snorted a final farewell.

We had the heebie-jeebies that whole day. Cautious eyes kept focus on the horizon as we shoveled load after load onto the gravel trucks. The last thing we wanted to see was another bear. Every snapping twig or movement in the brush caught our attention.

Now and then, one of us would recall something from the encounter. We talked it over, laughing nervously at both our actions and our stupidity.

"I guess that sergeant back at Camp Custer was right," Pick said. "There are bears up here, but we ain't seen no man-hungry moose or a crazy lumberjack ghost just yet."

"We best keep our eyes wide open from now on," Yasku said with a touch of fear in his voice. "The story about that crazy lumberjack ghost keeps me awake at night."

The walk back to camp that evening was full of good-natured joking. Still, we kept a close eye on the brush and trees alongside the road just in case our bear friend was in the area. When we got back to camp, we learned that Pick, Stosh, Yasku, and I were suddenly famous. The gravel truck drivers had spread the story of our wild animal encounter. Everyone in camp called us the Bear Hunters.

We enjoyed our newfound status. For some unknown reason, Mike was none too pleased.

FIFTEEN

AWOL

DAYS AND WEEKS PASSED WITHOUT MUCH CHANGING AT CAMP Polack Lake—until one night in June. Someone in our tent had the homesick blues. Boys aren't supposed to cry. Yet soft, whimpering sobs mixed with snoring in the darkness. There was no way of telling who it was. No one got up to offer support or comfort, not even me. I would come to regret that I didn't help a friend that night.

At 6:00 a.m., the morning whistle sounded. Yasku sat up on the edge of his cot and scratched his belly. Pick drew the covers over his head. "I say we snitch that whistle and bury it in the woods."

"Hey, where's Stosh?" I asked.

Pick pulled his covers down, sat up, and looked at the empty cot. "Maybe he's in the latrine."

The word *latrine* was another military term that we had come to use without a second thought. After some confusion, we discovered that a latrine was a community bathroom. Lieutenant Campbell told us it was a French word.

We dressed and made up our cots, leaving Stosh's the way we found it. Then we went off for our morning duties. Still no Stosh. Pick, Yasku, and I feared the worst. Our daily routine continued as if nothing happened. We had our flag raising and did our calisthenics—push-ups, sit-ups, jumping jacks. We policed the grounds, picking up scraps of paper and anything else that didn't belong. The captain insisted that his campsite be spotless.

After breakfast, we fell in for roll call. When Captain Mason called Stosh's name, there was nothing but silence.

Stosh's name was called again, louder.

"Maybe he's in the latrine, sir," I said hopefully.

"Go check up on him," the captain said as he continued the roll call.

I ran back to the latrine area. He wasn't there. Then I did a quick search behind the mess tent. No luck. When I reported back, the captain split up the work gangs and had us search the camp and the surrounding area. Stosh was nowhere to be found.

After our quick search, the camp reassembled for work detail. Once again my buddies and I picked up shovels and headed off to the gravel pit. Yasku spoke up to Mike. "Ain't we gonna keep looking for Stosh? He can't be far off."

Mike spun around to face us all. "No, we ain't gonna keep looking for Stosh," Mike said sarcastically. "Your buddy is

AWOL—you know, absent without leave. If and when your buddy comes back to camp, I'm going to recommend that he be kicked out of the CCC. Captain Mason will do it, too. He listens to me."

The morning walk to the gravel pit seemed much longer than usual. We walked in silence most of the way, looking desperately for any signs of Stosh. We held out some hope that he'd just wandered off and was somewhere near camp. But as hours passed, it was clear that he'd run off.

Pick spoke to me in Polish. He kept his voice down to a whisper so Mike couldn't hear. "We've got to do something. Maybe the bear got him. Even if he ran away, Stosh is sure to come to his senses sooner or later." His eyes studied me and the other guys. "When he does, he'll want his job back."

"Today the three of us will work as hard as four," I replied quietly in Polish. "We'll make up for Stosh's share. Tonight I'll talk to Captain Mason before Mike can get to him." Pick shared the plan with Yasku.

Through the day we worked harder than we had ever worked before. Mike gave his silent approval as we shoveled load after load into the endless line of gravel trucks. Our muscles screamed and our backs ached with strain. At the end of the day, we shuffled to camp, drained and bone-tired.

After a cold shower and a change to my dress clothes for supper, I walked over to Captain Mason's tent. I was scared, but there was no turning back. Stosh needed me, and my other buddies were counting on me.

SIXTEEN

Camp Commander

AS I APPROACHED HIS TENT, I COULD SEE THAT THE CAPTAIN'S head was down and he was focused on the paperwork in front of him. "Excuse me, Captain Mason," I said nervously as I stood at attention and saluted. "May I have a word with you?"

The captain returned my salute. "Stand at ease. What's your name, enrollee?

"Jarek Sokolowski, sir."

"What brings you here this afternoon, Sokolowski?" the captain asked as he straightened himself. He squared all the edges of his papers and files, placing them neatly on his desk. Then he lifted his gaze and looked me in the eye.

"My friend is Stoshu Campeau."

"Ah, the young man who went AWOL last night," the captain said as he turned and opened the top drawer of a file cabinet behind his desk. "Campeau ... Campeau," the captain muttered. "Here we go, let's see what we have."

Stosh's name was neatly lettered on the tab of the folder that Captain Mason retrieved. He opened it and examined the contents. His lips moved in silent speech as he read.

"Hmmm," the camp commander muttered as he stroked his chin. "It appears as though your friend has been placed on report several times by Assistant Leader O'Shea. The paperwork indicates that Campeau is a bit of a goldbrick. Now it seems he's deserted."

"S-s-sir," I explained nervously. "Stosh is only a little homesick. He's really a good worker. I'm sure he'll be back in camp in no time at all."

"Stosh . . . is that what you call your buddy?"

I nodded.

"Have you talked to Assistant Leader O'Shea about this matter?

"No, sir."

"Well, Sokolowski, I have to be straight with you. I don't like people who go AWOL. What's more, I made it perfectly clear that if enrollees have questions or problems, they're to talk with their assistant leaders, not me. Do you recall those instructions?"

"Yes, sir," I said weakly.

The captain picked up a pencil from his desktop and rolled it between his fingers. "President Roosevelt has given us jobs at a time when there aren't jobs to be had. When someone goes AWOL, like your friend Mr. Campeau, the CCC looks bad and I look bad. Worse yet, it makes the president look bad. Do you understand what I'm saying?"

"Yes, sir, I do. All of us know how important these jobs are. Our families are depending on us. It's just that Stosh has never been away before. He's just a little homesick, that's all. I am sure he'll be back tomorrow. The next day at the latest."

"Well, Sokolowski," the captain said as he closed Stosh's file and put it aside, "with Campeau's work record, I am not inclined to take him back. My first thought would be to discharge him and send him home."

My heart sank. I knew that Stosh needed this job. His family needed the money that the CCC sent each month. Stosh's father was sick. His mother had no job. And his brother and sister were hungry and suffering. I swallowed hard before continuing.

"Sir, I'll be responsible for Stosh when he returns. I'll make sure that his record is clean from this point forward. The guys in my work crew have agreed to pick up Stosh's share of the load until he gets back. When he comes back to camp, all I ask is that you give him another chance."

Captain Mason bounced the eraser end of the pencil on his desk as he thought. "You should have talked to Assistant Leader O'Shea about this matter. However, it took a lot of guts for you to come to me, Sokolowski. I admire that." The captain sat back in his swivel chair and leaned hard on his right elbow. "The CCC allows me a certain amount of discretion in these matters. So, if your friend comes back in a couple of days, I will consider taking him back. You see to it that your crew picks up Campeau's workload."

"Yes, sir, thank you, sir." I saluted awkwardly.

The captain returned the salute crisply. Then he shot me a serious look as he leaned forward. "Just make sure your crew picks up the slack. And one more thing, Sokolowski: from now on you are to report all matters to your assistant leader. Understand?"

"Yes, sir, I understand perfectly." I saluted the captain and left his quarters.

When I returned to my tent, I shared the news with the guys. We were all happy that the captain would give Stosh another chance once he came back to camp. Supper tasted extra good that night. Our spirits were high because we were certain that Stosh would return soon.

That night thunder rumbled off in the distance. We were headed for rough weather once again—and rougher times.

SEVENTEEN

The Storm

JUST BEFORE LIGHTS OUT, MIKE BURST INTO OUR TENT. THE violence of lightning was in his eyes, and thunder was in his voice. He scanned the tent and settled his attention on me. His chest rose and fell with each breath. Mike was seething with anger. "You!" he commanded as he pointed his finger at me, "Outside! Now!"

I knew I was about to get chewed out for going directly to the captain. Mike stormed out of the tent, and I followed him outside. Pick and Yasku looked at me sheepishly as I passed by their bunks and into the night. I half-expected that my friends would get up and follow me out of the tent in order to share Mike's rage, but that wasn't about to happen. The roll of thunder was coming closer and closer.

Once on the parade grounds, Mike turned to face me. His

fists clenched. "What gives you the right to go to the captain behind my back?"

"What? I didn't go behind your back." The lie tumbled out of my mouth. I knew full well that I had gone behind O'Shea's back. For some reason I wasn't willing to fess up to it.

Guys who were out for an evening stroll took to walking on the other side of the parade grounds when they heard Mike starting in on me. Here and there you could see heads popping out from underneath tent flaps. Those who enjoyed gossip would have a good story to tell in the morning.

"Well, mister, a chain of command exists in this outfit. It's pretty simple, even for an idiot like you." Mike poked his finger hard into my chest. "You don't go to the captain. Understand?" He poked me again, harder. "If you've got a question ... if you've got a problem ... if you've got a gripe ... you come to me. You don't go to the captain. I go to the captain. Got it?"

I scanned his eyes in the low light of nightfall. "I was just trying to help Stosh. That's all."

Mike grabbed me by the shirt with both hands. Rough arms pulled me close to his face. The smell of onions on his breath was sickening. "I don't like you. In fact, I don't like your little Polack buddies either. I should have cleaned your clock the first day I met you on the train. Now you go directly behind my back and beg the captain to save that lazy Stosh's job. Don't you ever go behind my back again."

"I-I-I was j-just trying to help my friend," I said. "I didn't mean any harm by it."

His anger shocked me. Mike shook me furiously, nearly ripping my clothes. "Listen and listen good," he said. "I don't care one iota about what you were trying to do. If you ever go to the captain again, I'll break you in two."

Mike bit off his words as he continued his rant. "Tonight I got chewed out by the lieutenant. You know why?"

I shook my head. "No."

"I got chewed out by the lieutenant because you went to the captain. The captain lambasted the lieutenant because you didn't follow the chain of command. The lieutenant took some of my hide because you didn't follow the chain of command. Now it's my turn to pass along some wisdom and a warning to you."

He turned his head and focused his right eye on me. "If you and your buddies think you've had it rough so far, I got news for you. I'm gonna do everything I can to make your lives miserable. You'll have the jobs nobody wants. I'm gonna work you like dogs. Wait and see. You're gonna beg me to kick you out of the CCC. And if you screw up even one time, I'll have you on the next train back to Polack town whether you want to go back or not."

O'Shea twisted his head and looked at me closely. "That's funny ain't it? Jarek Sokolowski gets kicked out of the CCC at Camp Polack Lake and is sent home to Polack town." He laughed deeply, then suddenly turned silent and serious. Mike released one hand and balled it into a fist in front of my face. "Do you understand me, or do I have to explain myself further?"

"I understand. You don't need to explain any further."

He released me and stomped off into the night. As I gathered myself, I noticed guys pulling their heads in and closing tent flaps. Lightning lit the sky and the clouds opened up. Rain fell in buckets. The real storm was yet to strike.

Mike was right. I was wrong. Still in all, no matter how much talking or going through proper channels I would have done, Mike had proven over and over that he wouldn't listen to my side of an argument. It would have been useless for me to take this problem to Mike. He had given me no choice but to go directly to the captain. Still, he didn't see it that way.

I didn't follow the proper chain of command. So, I was on the hot seat. What made me mad was how Mike O'Shea handled the problem.

EIGHTEEN

Hard Rain

IT HAD BEEN RAINING AROUND THE CLOCK SINCE I HAD GOTTEN my chain-of-command lecture from Mike O'Shea. Stosh had been gone three long days. Sunup tomorrow would be day four. Captain Mason told me he might allow him back if he returned in a couple days. By most accounts, a couple means two. Stosh was stretching his luck. What's more, all of us were exhausted from picking up his slack.

After lights out, I laid in my cot thinking. Though I was dog tired and arm weary, I couldn't sleep. The rain was coming in waves. A leak at the top of the center pole kept up a rhythmic drip of raindrops on the floor. Thoughts kept running through my mind.

Drip. Drip. Drip.

I thought about Mike and our last run-in. Mike O'Shea

was bigger, older, and stronger than me. The way I figured it, he'd been a bully most of his life. I had been warned about people like him. My father told me that the only way to stop bullies was to stand up to them. I wasn't afraid to fight Mike if it came to that.

My father was a great boxer in his time. Once he even fought Stanley Ketchell, the Polish boxer from Grand Rapids who won the world middleweight championship in 1908. Father gave up his dream to be a professional boxer after that fight. He got married and settled down, taking a job in a furniture factory until he was laid off in 1931.

From the time we were little, our father taught both Squint and me how to box. He built a boxing ring with cotton rope in the backyard and showed us how to defend ourselves. We learned how to punch and duck, to use our legs as well as our arms to deliver a punch. Squint never really took to the sport. Maybe it was because his eyesight was so bad. On the other hand, I got pretty good at it. Though I was never really interested in brawling in the alleys with other boys, I enjoyed boxing. In local tournaments I went undefeated for two straight years.

Though the prospect of fighting with Mike didn't bother me much, I was worried about the outcome—one way or the other. If I lost, Big Mike would rub my nose in the fact he had beaten me. If I won, Big Mike would continue to bait me into a re-match or use his position in the CCC to beat me down.

Drip. Drip. Drip.

I was worried that if I fought with Mike, I might get kicked out of the Civilian Conservation Corps. Part of the

Oath of Enrollment talked about obeying rules and following the orders of superiors. Clearly Big Mike was a superior,
and the captain and lieutenant established the rule that they
didn't want any fighting.

The CCC was more than a job. It was life, life for my
whole family. My sister had written several times since I
arrived at Camp Polack Lake. Squint and our father were
still looking for work, but it didn't look like things would
change for some time. Sophia was a maid for a doctor and
his wife. Though she worked many hours a week, the job only
paid $4 a month—not nearly enough. The doctor wanted to
pay her more, but could not. Most people were so poor they
would pay him with a chicken or some potatoes for mending
a broken leg or delivering a baby.

Back at home, the mayor and the governor worked hard
to provide shelter and food for the starving people of Grand
Rapids. My family got handouts from time to time, but they
didn't like being on the dole. It was clear that they were living
off the $25 that the CCC sent to them each month. I had no
choice. I was trapped. I couldn't risk my job by fighting with
Mike. Regardless of what happened, I had to put up with his
taunts and cruelty. What's worse, he knew that he had me
trapped. I even suspect he enjoyed it.

Drip. Drip. Drip.

Pick and Yasku were snoring loudly. Why was I the one
who was awake? I wondered why I carried these burdens,
and no one else seemed to have a care in the world. I was
the youngest among my friends. Why was I the one to go to
Captain Mason? The more I thought, the more unsettled I

grew. I had to get some sleep. Tomorrow would come soon enough.

The cold, hard rain that had gone on since Stosh had left made a bad job worse. I thought about the pit and dreaded working there and working for O'Shea. The rain was filling the pit with icy cold water making each shovelful of gravel that much heavier. Cold rainwater ran down our arms and backs as we worked. In the pit, our feet got so numb that we couldn't feel them when we walked. We often stumbled when throwing gravel into the trucks. It was getting dangerous. Someone was going to get hurt—and hurt bad.

I finally fell asleep late that rainy night. Before sunup I woke with a start, feeling as though eyes were staring at me from out of the dark.

Stosh had come back.

NINETEEN

The Prodigal

AT FIRST I THOUGHT I WAS DREAMING. AFTER I SHOOK MYSELF awake, I realized that it really was Stosh, but he looked different. He looked more like a drowned rat than my old friend. His clothes were tattered and soaked, and he shivered from cold. His face and hands were blue and swollen.

Stosh could barely speak. "J-J-J-Jarek," he whispered hoarsely. "He-he-he-help m-m-me." His body shook with each word.

"Get those wet things off," I said as I threw off my covers and rolled out of my cot. "You need to put some warm things on." I wrapped blankets around him and rubbed the cold out of his back. The others began stirring. "Get Stosh's other clothes," I said to Yasku. Then I turned to Pick. "Run to the mess tent and get some hot coffee ... fast." The other guys in the tent wanted to help, too. Everyone was glad that Stosh was back.

Thankfully, it was Saturday and there was no work detail. We wouldn't have to report for duty until Monday morning. As we dried Stosh off and warmed him, I thought about what we should do to help him keep his job. Taking him directly to Captain Mason would be like stirring a hornet's nest. We'd have to report his return to Mike. From there we could only hope that Captain Mason would take him back in the CCC. I had done all I could. Stosh's fate was now in the hands of others.

As he warmed and regained his strength, Stosh told us that he had been trying to go home. Fortunately or unfortunately, he never made it to Manistique before turning back. He was hungry, tired, and had cuts all over his face and arms. When Pick came back with coffee, he brought along sweet rolls. They were still warm.

Stosh wolfed down the rolls and took a sip of coffee. "This cup of mud sure tastes good, I'll tell you," Stosh said as he lifted his coffee cup before sharing his story. His color slowly returned and the shivering had stopped.

"Sorry if I caused you guys to worry, but I just wanted to go home for a while. When I left in the night, I thought I'd head for Manistique to try to catch a boat that would take me home, but I kept getting lost. I never got anywhere near a town."

Stosh looked at us from the warm covering of his blanket. He slurped more coffee before continuing. "First off, I found a stream that I thought would take me southeast toward Lake Michigan. Instead, it took me deep into a swamp where I spent the first night," Stosh said as he shook his head. "The rain and the cold and the bugs almost drove me crazy. I stumbled into a stream once and came out covered in leeches."

The next day, he said, he found a road. "I thought maybe I could hitch a ride to town, but no cars, trucks or horses came along," he continued. "I was so hungry, cold, and sore that I almost gave up then and there." Stosh took a long pull off his cup. "Yesterday morning, a truck came along. I got a ride and a piece of bread. Once I got some food in my belly, I started thinking a little more clearly."

"What do you mean?" I asked.

"This is hard work, and we're all a long way from home," Stosh replied. "But being in the CCC is a lot better than being on your own. Maybe I would have made it home in a week or so. Maybe I would've gotten lost and died of starvation. Who knows? I might've gotten eaten by a bear or a moose out there."

Stosh looked around at all of the guys in the tent. "Those nights in the cold rain made me realize that my life wasn't the only thing I was risking by running off. My family is counting on me for their survival. If I die, they may be dead, too. Taking off like that was foolish. Now I only hope that it isn't too late to beg for forgiveness and get my job back." Stosh hung his head low.

"Did ya see the crazy lumberjack ghost?" Yasku asked. "I been hoping that you wouldn't run into that guy."

"Nah," Stosh said. "Being out in this wilderness alone was scary enough for me, though."

Pick put his hand on Stosh's shoulder. "Jarek went to

Captain Mason just after you left. It took a lot for him to do that. In fact, everybody in camp knows that it got him in big trouble with Mike." The other guys nodded in agreement. "The three of us have been doing the work of four since you've been gone. We're with you, Stosh. Now it's up to you to earn your job back."

Ben, one of the other guys in the tent, spoke up. "We're all with you, Stosh." The others agreed. "Let's all go see Captain Mason." The guys turned and headed for the tent door.

"Not so fast," I said. "If we go to the captain on this, we'll all suffer." I hesitated before continuing. "There's only one way to do this. Stosh and I have to go to Mike."

Stosh stood up and steeled himself for what was ahead.

Broken Chain

BY MID-MORNING, STOSH WAS FEELING BETTER. HIS HEAD, hands, and arms were covered in welts and cuts. After more food and coffee, he started joking around like the Stosh we all knew. It was time to visit Mike. We found him in the first place we looked, the mess tent.

Mike looked up from a comic book he was reading and did a double take. An evil smile crept across his face. "Well, well, well," he began. "Did little Stoshy run home to mommy? Let me hear you cry, you baby."

"That's enough, Mike." I said. "I'm following the chain of command by reporting in to you. Stosh made a mistake. Now he's back."

"So he is," Mike said, looking at his fingernails. "So he is. And as far as you finally following the proper chain of command, you've proven me wrong about something."

"What's that?" I asked with a skeptical glare.

"I thought you were too stupid to learn anything," Mike sneered. "I might have been wrong about that, but don't go telling anybody. It sure sounds like you've learned a lesson about following the proper chain of command." Mike stretched his arms wide and arched his back. Then he cracked his knuckles loudly before continuing. "Like I said before, I'll recommend to Captain Mason that your little buddy here be discharged and sent home immediately."

I held myself back from throttling Mike. "Wait a minute," I started. "Captain Mason told me that he would at least consider giving Stosh his job back if he came back in a couple of days. He's back, and he's ready to start work."

"Right," Mike said. "The good captain said that if Stosh came back in a couple of days, he'd consider keeping him on in the Cs. By my count, today is four days after your wet-nosed buddy here went AWOL. That's more than a couple of days. My recommendation to Captain Mason will be as I have told you." Mike looked me in the eyes. "If you push this any further or go behind my back again, I'll see to it that you face disciplinary action. So get out of my sight before I come down on the two of you like a ton of bricks." Mike turned away, dismissing the conversation.

Stosh was crestfallen. We walked back to our tent in silence. Before going inside he turned to me. "Jarek, I appreciate all you've done for me. I do. But you need to take care of yourself and your family. Just let me take things from here by myself."

"I can't do that, Stosh," I said. "We need to stick together.

We can't let a guy like Mike win in this situation. There's got to be something more we can do. I need time to clear my head and think." An idea occurred to me. "One of the supply trucks will be taking a tour of work projects, then heading to town for a few hours. What say we go for a ride?"

The rain cleared off later that morning, and the sky opened for the first time in days. Right after lunch, we headed out for a tour and a day of rest and relaxation. A cloud of blue smoke belched out of the old truck as the driver fired up the engine. About a dozen guys climbed into the back and took seats on the rigid planks.

The driver revved the engine and ground the transmission into first gear. The tired old vehicle slowly came to life and limped forward. As it was picking up speed, one of the boys from camp started running toward us. The guys cheered, encouraging him to run faster. He was gaining just as the driver shifted to second and began pulling away. Though he started falling behind, the runner kept coming. Miraculously, the truck backfired and slowed a bit. It was just enough for the runner to close the gap.

I grabbed the side rail and stepped on the back bumper, reaching out as far as I could. When the runner and I clasped hands, I pulled with all my might. The others took hold of me and helped. We dragged him aboard safely. It was Ben, one of the guys from our tent.

Once he took his place on the plank seat, Ben wiped his brow. "Thanks for the hand. I wasn't sure I was going to make it," he said, gasping for air. "I wanted to tell you the good news."

"Good news? I could use a little good news about now. What is it?" I asked.

"I told my assistant leader about the trouble you're having with Mike." Ben said between deep breaths. "He told me he'd talk to Captain Mason about Stosh. You know, coming back and wanting his job and all."

That day we toured the miles of road that were being built with the gravel we dug. We also saw fire trails through the woods, a couple of fire watch towers that stood guard over tall ridges, and the telephone lines that connected the towers to the camp. We all shared a sense of pride. We also made a stop at another CCC camp that was to the east of Polack Lake.

After picking up a few more riders, we took off for Manistique and saw a picture show. It cost us each a whole two bits, but it was worth it. The movie was *Duck Soup*, and it featured the Marx brothers. We laughed our cares away for a time.

It was a great day. Still, worry hung over me. Mike wouldn't be happy about another assistant leader talking to Captain Mason about Stosh. He would see it as going behind his back once again.

We were headed for a showdown.

TWENTY-ONE

The Turn

THE WEEKEND CAME AND WENT WITHOUT A WORD FROM MIKE, Lieutenant Campbell, or Captain Mason. We waited on pins and needles. It was like we were hunkered down for an explosion that never came. At roll call on Monday morning, Captain Mason called Stosh's name as usual. This time Stosh shouted "Here!" and his name was given a check mark on the clipboard. It was a reply that hadn't been heard in camp since early in the week before, yet no one commented on his return. Still, we waited for some kind of response or speech about going AWOL. There was nothing, not a peep.

After we were issued our shovels from the tool shed, we headed for the pit just like any other day. Mike never said a word, good or bad. We walked in silence for fear of breaking the spell. We waited for an outburst that didn't come—at least, not yet.

97

Michigan's Upper Peninsula is a land of extremes. The weather had taken a dramatic turn for the better. The previous week had felt like the return of fall. Today it was like spring had been skipped altogether; the northland was suddenly immersed in full-blown summer. We got rid of our hats and shirts as we labored under the hot sun.

The work crew kept up a good pace, even after a cloud of bugs showed up. Early summer is black fly season in the U.P.—and black flies are sneaky and nasty. They land softly and like to nibble people behind the ears, at the hairline, and where clothing fits snugly against the body. After black flies finish feeding on human flesh, they often leave a trail.

I noticed blood running down the back of Yasku's neck. "Did ya cut yourself?" I asked.

"Naw, don't think so," Yasku responded. He reached back to scratch behind his ear and came away with blood on his fingertips. The trail down his neck came from a small red bump that was beginning to swell. It was the same kind of bug bite that had covered Stosh's head and arms when he spent days in the swamps of northern Michigan. The pit was bad enough. Now the bugs were making matters much worse.

At midday, Mike arrived on the beat-up supply truck that was delivering lunch. The old rattletrap pulled away after dropping off its cargo and passenger. I tried not to pay any attention to Mike as we ate our sandwiches. He sat on a stump, pulled out a pocket knife, and began cutting an apple. Mike carefully sliced it and balanced each piece on the blade as he ate. When he finished, he studied the core for a moment. Without warning he reached back and threw it with all the power he had. The juicy core hit me on the side of the head.

I lost my temper and closed the distance between him and me. Before I could throw myself into a fight, Pick and Yasku grabbed me. Stosh shrank back, afraid to get involved. I kicked and screamed, struggling against my friends. The weeks and months of abuse had come to a boil. Mike needed to be taught a lesson, and I was mad enough to teach it.

"Calm down," Yasku shouted in Polish as he shook me in his grip.

"C'mon, Polack," Mike said taunting me with his arms at his side. "Stop talking that pig Latin with your buddies and hit me. I know you want to. So, go ahead."

Pick turned me roughly toward him. "Don't do it, Jarek. He's looking for an excuse to fight."

"That's it," Yasku said. "He only wants to get you kicked out of the CCC."

Yasku's words got through to me. It made sense. Mike wanted to get into a fight so he could report me for misconduct or for punching a superior. I straightened up and relaxed my arms. Yasku and Pick loosened their grip.

"It's time to get back to work, boys," I said to my friends. We all picked up our shovels and headed back down into the pit.

Mike leaned hard against the truck as we loaded gravel into it. He wiped his mouth on the back of his sleeve. Then he sauntered down into the pit and spoke to me so no one else could hear. "Too bad, Polack! You missed your chance. You see, I want to stomp you like a bug, but if I hit you first

... well, let's just say I like my job and I want to keep it. You went behind my back again, and you're gonna pay dearly. I don't know when, and I don't know where, but one day I will beat the daylights out of you."

I gripped my shovel hard, knuckles whitened under the pressure. Mike laughed and climbed the side of the pit. Before leaving, he turned. "Oh, I almost forgot why I came here." He waited until we all stopped working to hear his announcement. "Campeau, report for KP once you get back to camp. Sokolowski, join your pal this evening and for the rest of the week."

After we returned from another day in the pit, we reported for KP. Stosh and I were fortunate enough to get the firewood detail as our duty. Cook stoves and dishwater were heated with wood fires. Each evening, piles of wood were cut, split, and stacked for the following day. It wasn't the worst of the jobs and it was better than scrubbing pots and doing dishes, but it was humiliating pulling KP detail along with all the goof-offs in camp.

After supper that night, Yasku and I scratched our bug bites and played cards on my bunk. Just before lights-out, Pick and Ben came roaring into the tent. They fell onto their cots and pulled pillows over their faces to muffle their laughter. Once their beds stopped shaking, they looked at each other and started laughing all over again.

"What's so funny?" I asked out of curiosity.

Pick spoke just above a whisper, "Mike had a visitor tonight."

"A visitor, really? Who was it?" asked Yasku, slapping a card on top of mine.

"That visitor was a skunk," Ben chuckled. "Mike O'Shea and everything he owns stink to high heaven. Now nobody, but nobody, wants to get near him. The best thing is no one, not even Mike, has a clue as to how that friendly little skunk happened to find its way in there."

"You should've seen him trying to shoo that skunk out of his tent," Pick snorted. "The most wonderful part of the story is that only Ben and I know how the little stinker got in there in the first place."

TWENTY-TWO

Sign of Deer

July 1934

AS THE SUMMER WORE ON, AN ARMY CREW CAME AROUND and built real wooden barracks at Camp Polack Lake. The black tarpaper that covered the exterior of the buildings was far from beautiful. The inside was as plain and simple as a cardboard box with a couple of windows. Still, the barracks had comfortable beds and gave us shelter from rain and bugs. It was a welcome change from tent life.

In addition to the barracks, Polack Lake now had a recreation hall with a meager library and an infirmary for treating illnesses and wounds. Quarters were also constructed for officers, the forester, and the local experienced men who were hired to help us CCC boys learn different jobs. Polack Lake was no longer a campsite. It was a community.

Life in the wilderness had fallen into a routine of

getting up early, flag raising, morning exercises, policing the grounds, breakfast, inspection, roll call, grabbing tools, walking to work, shoveling gravel, then returning for dinner, followed by a few hours of free time before sleep. To fill the evening hours, classes were offered in the rec hall. Despite Mike's opposition, I signed up to take motor vehicle operations. The schooling helped keep my dream of being a truck driver alive. The routine continued until the early morning hours of one hot, hazy July day.

During calisthenics, five deer broke through the brush that grew around our camp. The deer scurried past our formation, bouncing and zigzagging off to the far side of the parade grounds. It was a beautiful, graceful sight. We took it as a good sign. Before the day was over, we would learn otherwise.

Andy Timmons had been nicknamed King Kong because he could climb faster and higher than anyone at camp, so he was our fire ranger. Each day he watched the forest from atop a 140-foot tower at the top of a hill a couple of miles west of the lake. Most of the guys in camp envied him because his job was so easy. All he had to do was stay awake and keep a lookout.

King Kong climbed the ladder to the top of the fire tower right after breakfast that particular July morning. There was a gray haze out to the west, but that wasn't uncommon. Low-lying fog and storm clouds often presented themselves as gray lines on the horizon. From atop his tower, he saw a parade of animals—deer, possum, skunk, and raccoon. It wasn't uncommon for him to see wildlife from his perch, but today was different. He'd never seen the woods so alive with life. Animals seemed to be running with purpose. What had gotten into them?

After a time, he carefully studied the horizon with his binoculars. He lowered them slowly and rubbed his eyes. Then he raised them a second time to make sure of what he was seeing. King Kong couldn't believe his eyes. Hands shaking, he cranked the generator on the telephone in the tower.

"Captain," he said nervously, "we've got a wildfire."

King Kong put down the phone and took another look at the fire through his binoculars. Then he checked the windsock that inflated in the breeze above his head before picking up the phone once again.

"Yes sir, the fire is west-southwest at 240 degrees. I'd estimate that it's eight to ten miles away. Wind speed is ten to fifteen miles per hour out of the southwest. Yes, that's right. Oh, and sir, it looks like it's moving fast."

Trucks gathered us up from our work sites around camp. Though we'd been given some training in how to fight a wildfire and we'd had some practice drills, this was the real thing. The trucks rumbled down gravel roads and two-lane ruts. Old vehicles were pushed to their limits. Guided by the compass heading that King Kong had given, we traveled the twisting roads up ridges and down valleys. It was easy to tell that we were getting close to the fire; the smoke was nearly suffocating.

Stosh, Pick, Yasku, and I were assigned a portion of the line that was near the south end of the fire. Handkerchiefs covered our faces. The work was both simple and hard. Axes, picks, grub hoes, and shovels were used to cut a line in the ground that we hoped the fire would not cross. Our backs supplied the energy.

To create a break, we had to clear all brush, timber, and grass in the path of the fire. If we could get the work done in time, we would use drip torches to light a backfire, which could eliminate some of the fire's fuel and widen the break we were making. This way, we could actually fight fire with fire. The hope was that with some luck, we could stop the wildfire in its tracks.

That day we learned that a wildfire is a living, breathing beast—a creature with a mind of its own. We strained to cut the fire line. The beast was a couple of miles off when we started working. As it charged toward us, it threw off smoke and heat. Sweat poured down our backs and off our brows. Soot and ash covered us from head to toe. As it approached, the roar was deafening.

We did the best we could to stay ahead of it. As the beast drew near, flames licked at the margins of the line. When the wind kicked up, it roared at us, spewing fire and flaming embers. We fell back to escape the heat, fighting as we retreated. Our focus was on the ground immediately ahead, furiously clearing anything that would feed it.

We couldn't stop the creature. The fire easily jumped the line we made and was overtaking us.

TWENTY-THREE

Fire and Ice
July 1934

"RUN FOR IT!" I SHOUTED AT THE TOP OF MY LUNGS. MY VOICE was barely heard over the roar.

It was move or die. I tapped each guy on the shoulder to get their attention. We dropped our tools and picked our way through slashings, stumps, brush piles, and fallen timber to make our escape.

The beast clawed at our heels as we struggled to keep ahead of it. Lungs were bursting as we ran. Barbs and branches tore at our skin. Eventually we found our way to the rim of a valley. There was a small stream that flowed down below.

"This way! The stream has to lead somewhere!" I called out. Looking back, I saw that more guys had fallen in behind us and were running for their very lives.

Stosh made an attempt to go down into the valley, but it was clogged with downed trees and heaped with dead branches and thorn bushes. We quickly picked up a deer trail that followed the general direction of the valley floor. The group pushed forward. Our mouths were dry and our legs were so tired they felt like stumps. Each person took a turn in the lead, breaking the trail and looking for any way of escape. The beast roared behind us without letup, snapping and growling in anger.

The deer trail took a sudden turn away from the stream and up a rise. As we topped the hill, a small lake stretched out before us. We stumbled down the hill toward the safety of the water. Yasku and Pick stayed behind to help some of the guys who had fallen back. One was coughing uncontrollably, another had a bum leg.

One by one, we fell into the water. One by one, we started screaming. The spring-fed lake was ice cold. Our bodies were being cooked by a wildfire; our legs were freezing in a lake. We stood shivering in the water as the beast approached. It took time, but we adjusted to the water temperature. We were glad to be alive.

I took a head count. There were twenty-two of us in the lake, but we weren't alone. Animals of all varieties joined us—deer, raccoon, opossum, skunk. For the moment, we were all safe in our common refuge, man and animal. The beast growled. As it approached, we went deeper and deeper into the water. The wildfire surrounded the small lake, then swept off.

Eventually we emerged from the icy water. Lips were

blue and teeth chattered uncontrollably. Beneath our feet, the ground was hot. Everything within eyesight was burned black. Here and there, skeletons of scrub brush, scraggly hardwood trees, stumps, and deadfalls flickered with small fires. Smoke hung low to the ground. Nightfall was near at hand. That day felt like it had come and gone in only a few moments, a few breaths. Wet clothes and the chill that swept over us at sundown made the night seem much longer.

I checked on each of the guys from time to time. It was hard to recognize anyone in the dark. The job was harder still because our faces were covered in soot and ash. One of the guys stayed awake the entire night. It was only when he spoke that I recognized it was Ben.

"That's what it was like, Jarek," Ben said. "That's what it was like."

"What are you talking about?" I asked.

Ben and a couple of other guys in camp had come from northern Wisconsin, an area north of Green Bay. He sat there in the dark rocking back and forth. Only his eyes were visible. The story he told added another layer of chill to the night.

"Back home in Peshtigo they tell about a firestorm that took the whole town in 1871. People there say that the fire took place the same time as the great Chicago fire, only it was worse. In a single night, the whole town was nothing but cinder ash. Some say that more than two thousand people were killed by that fire."

Ben swallowed hard. "Jarek, we could've been killed today—burned alive just like some of my relatives in Peshtigo."

I did the best I could to comfort him, but he wasn't the only one who was shaken by the awesome power of the wildfire we fought that day. Most of us didn't get any sleep at all that night. Trails of sooty tears and sweat traced the ridgelines of our faces. Hair was singed off our arms, eyebrows, and heads. We were cut and bruised. Just before sunup, a steady rain began to beat down on us. Hot embers sizzled at the touch of rain.

In the early light, we retraced our steps from the day before, following the ridgeline of the valley and searching for remembered landmarks in the devastated countryside. Eventually Stosh found a shovel. Its handle was charred, but it was still useable.

As we followed the burned-out fire line north, we heard the sound of voices calling out from across the wasteland. A few of the boys tended to the others while Pick ran off to find the rescue-and-recovery team. We were to discover that the beast consumed about a thousand acres of the Marquette National Forest.

The CCC nearly had the fire under control, but it was the rain that saved the day.

TWENTY-FOUR

News from Home
July 1934

A TRUCK CARRIED US BACK TO CAMP LATE IN THE MORNING.
Those of us who jumped into the lake to avoid the fire had
been the last to return. Friends cheered as we arrived.
Though everyone was eager to find out how we managed to
survive, we couldn't wait to get cleaned up and into fresh
clothes. A shower had never felt so good. After we scrubbed
the soot and smell off ourselves, we headed to the mess hall
for some chow. Cookie made goulash. The food tasted smoky,
but we ate like it was our last meal. No one had been seriously
injured while fighting the fire. We were thankful for that.

Before going back to the barracks for some sack time,
I checked in at the recreation hall. I was one of the lucky
ones. There was mail from home. Mother and Father did
not read or write English. Squint didn't like to write much,

probably because his vision was so poor. However, my sister Sophia wrote to me each week. I tried to write back as often as I could.

I took the letter to my bunk, where I read it eagerly. My parents were doing fine. Father was looking for work, but prospects weren't good. Sophia still had her job as a maid. Between what she earned and the money that was sent home from the CCC, my family was getting by with few frills.

Her letter was filled with well-wishes from close friends and people from the parish. She wrote about old neighbors who had moved out and some who had moved in. Then she got to the point of her letter. I read in stunned silence, not wanting to believe the message. My face must have told the story. I lowered the paper and covered my eyes.

Yasku was eating a candy bar when he took notice of me and edged his way to my bunk.

"Sumpin' wrong?" he asked as he munched his treat.

"Squint's dead," I replied hoarsely.

"Nah, that can't be!"

"Squint was never the same after he washed out of the CCC," I said as I stared at the ceiling. "When he got back home he felt guilty, said he was being a burden on our family."

I took a deep breath and crushed the letter. "He heard there was work out West. So, he took up with hobo ways, hopping trains and begging for handouts as he headed out to California."

"How'd he die?"

"Sophia said that a railroad bull beat him up and tossed him off a train outside of Kansas City."

"A railroad bull killed him?" Yasku asked, horrified.

"Not directly," I replied as I rubbed my forehead. "The bull that caught Squint freeloading a ride on the train roughed him up pretty bad. Those men can be heartless. A couple of hobos riding the train with Squint managed to keep the bull from killing him. But they all got thrown off the train.

"Anyway, Squint survived the bull's beating and spent a few days in a hobo jungle to recover from his injuries. But when he tried to hop a westbound a few days later, Squint didn't have the strength to hold on. He lost his grip on the car and fell underneath the train." I hesitated before continuing, staring blankly at the ceiling. "He was killed instantly. Squint always kept his home address on a card in his pocket. My family got a letter from the police."

I didn't tell Yasku the rest of the story. It was too personal. My parents didn't have the money to go out to Kansas or to send his body home. Instead, he was buried out there in a cemetery with a simple wooden cross for a headstone.

The sorrow and sadness were like a fog that sat heavily on my chest. While in the CCC, I missed home as much as anyone else. Still, I missed Squint most of all. Now he was gone forever. There was a hole in my life that would never be filled. I hadn't even had the chance to say a proper good-bye.

Yasku was without words. All he could do was whisper simple thoughts of sympathy. Unconsciously, he knew the right thing to do. He placed his hand on my shoulder and walked quietly away to leave me with my thoughts.

I had a sudden urge to get moving. I needed time to think. The day had cleared up after the morning shower. As I paced the parade grounds, mud caked my shoes. It didn't matter; there was only one thing on my mind. My brother had always been special to me. He had been more than a friend. Sure, we'd our share of troubles. Still, he was the one person who would always stand up for me. It didn't matter if I was right or wrong. Squint was a friend, tried and true.

As I paced thinking things through, Yasku was blabbing to everyone in camp that my brother had died. He made no mention that Squint was the fella who had washed out of the CCC only a few months back. He just wanted to let people know that I was suffering.

Ambling back and forth, I was lost in sadness and regret. Deep thoughts and remembrances haunted me. A hard shot to my shoulder shocked me to my senses.

"Watch it," grunted Mike.

TWENTY-FIVE

Fighting Words

July 1934

"LEAVE ME ALONE," I HISSED. "I DON'T WANT ANY OF YOUR guff today."

"Well," Mike said, "isn't that just too bad." He circled around to face me. "I've got a bone to pick with you."

"Not now." I turned to walk away.

"Yeah, now!" Mike grabbed me by the upper arm and spun me around. "Don't walk away from me. What's with you Polacks? Are you all cowards?"

"What are you talking about?" My anger started to boil over.

"Yesterday at the fire, you and your buddies turned tail and ran when things got a little hot," he mocked. "If you'd stuck it out like men, we would have had that fire under control. Instead, you ran away."

115

"You don't know what you're talking about," I said squaring up to Mike. "We had no choice. If we'd stayed, a lot of good men would have been hurt or killed. Besides, I didn't see you pitching in to help when the fire jumped the line and started racing toward us."

He leaned forward, sputtering with anger. "Bear hunters? Baloney! I knew the first day I met you Polacks that you were all chicken livers."

I went red with rage tackling Mike to the ground. We rolled around in the dirt, each struggling to get the advantage. I got him in a headlock, but he managed to wiggle free. Finally, we broke away from each other and put up our fists, then began circling for a fight.

"I been looking forward to this," Mike said through his clenched teeth. "You're gonna get what you got coming."

A small voice in the back of my head was telling me to cool off and back down, but I wasn't in the mood to listen to that voice. O'Shea was the one who threw the apple at Squint. O'Shea was the one who was making life miserable for me and my buddies. I'd just lost my only brother. Now Mike kept pushing. It was time for me to push back for a change.

"I'm gonna feed you a knuckle sandwich, O'Shea. Just tell me when you've had your fill."

I moved my head to the left and threw a right to his midsection. The punch knocked the wind out of O'Shea. His eyes bulged as his arms drew into his chest. I moved right and gave him a shot in the ribs. He gasped again. Then I moved back and covered up, thinking that O'Shea would come after me with all he had. When he did, I was going to stop his charge and bust him good.

"Break it up!" Lieutenant Campbell shouted as he pushed us apart.

Mike pointed an accusing finger at me. "He started it. You saw it all, didn't you? He tackled me. He punched me first. He attacked a superior. I was just defending myself."

The lieutenant looked at Mike. "I don't care who started it. There's been a rub between you two boys for a long time. I've seen it, and I'm tired of it. We're gonna finish this matter once and for all right after the morning whistle tomorrow. Until then, stay away from each other."

I stared Mike down for a moment. It was clear that I'd hurt him in our quick fight. His anger simmered as the lieutenant's words sunk in.

Not wanting to go against the lieutenant, O'Shea turned away and started mumbling about something. I brushed the dust and dirt from my clothes and headed back to the barracks. That afternoon a lot of guys came by to say a few kind words to me about losing my brother. I guess Yasku thought he was doing the right thing by telling everyone about Squint, but I wished he'd kept his trap shut.

Rumors about my fight with Mike were also circulating. The entire camp had heard about how I stood up to O'Shea and put in a couple of good licks. A few fellas said that it took guts to fight Big Mike. Some gave advice. All of them told me to punch his lights out.

I wasn't proud of my scrap with O'Shea. I've always looked at boxing as one thing, and street fighting as another. My temper had gotten the best of me that afternoon. I wasn't happy about that. Though it only lasted seconds, the fight had taught me a few things. Above all, I learned that my weeks in the pit shoveling gravel had put some muscle on my bones. I wasn't the skinny cat who'd joined the CCC.

I had no appetite for supper that night. I was sick about the news from home, and I was sick and tired of the way Mike treated me. And, truth be known, I was embarrassed at my outburst with O'Shea. The events of the day stayed with me during my class in motor vehicle operations. One of the drivers showed us how to work the clutch and shift through the gears. Though I sat in the seat and ran through the practice, my mind was elsewhere. It was hard for me to hold on to anything . . . It was even hard for me to hold on to my dream of being a truck driver. My run-in with Mike hadn't helped things.

Lieutenant Campbell said that Mike and I were going to settle things once and for all. That was fine by me. There was a lot of anger I had to get off my chest. As I lay in my bunk that night, I punched Mike in the nose over and over in my dreams.

My time had come.

TWENTY-SIX

Gloves

July 1934

THE REVEILLE WHISTLE BLEW AT 6:00 A.M., JUST LIKE ANY other workday at Polack Lake. We fell into formation for morning exercises. Lieutenant Campbell had another idea.

"This morning," the lieutenant began, "we're going to settle a dispute between O'Shea and Sokolowski." He formed the enrollees in a large circle and told Mike and me to stand on the inside of it. Lieutenant Campbell cut through the ring of boys. He was carrying a large army duffle. He opened the bag and dumped the contents out onto the ground.

Boxing gloves. Two sets of eight-ouncers. They were old and worn like the ones Father had hanging from the rafters in our basement back in Grand Rapids. The gloves were dirty and dusty. Cracks in the leather of the gloves would open cuts on the fighters' faces. I didn't care. This was my chance to get back at Mike O'Shea, and I was looking forward to it.

The lieutenant looked at us. "Put 'em on, boys. Have your buddies help you lace 'em up. Make sure they're tight, so they don't come off during the fight."

The rules were simple. We were to box three-minute rounds with a minute of rest between each round. Lieutenant Campbell would referee. The first to be knocked out or to call it quits would be the loser.

Stosh helped me with my gloves. "Watch out, Jarek. He's big, and he's strong."

"That doesn't matter," I said. "I'm going to pound him into the ground. My father taught me how to handle a mug like him. You watch."

Mike and I joined in the center of the ring. The lieutenant held out his right arm to separate us. Once he was sure we were ready to go, he said one word: "Box!"

I went at Mike with all I had. My anger took over and I swung at him wildly, putting aside everything I had learned about boxing. My arms spun like a windmill at O'Shea, but nothing landed. The guys who formed the ring were shouting and cat-calling. Mike stepped forward, wrapped his arms around me, and threw me to the ground like a sack of potatoes. Immediately, Lieutenant Campbell pulled us to our feet and pushed us apart.

"Box!"

I came to my senses and started to box like I had been taught. Instead of rushing in to work him over, I circled, waiting for an opening. This frustrated Mike. He held out his hands and taunted, "C'mon, you coward, fight."

That's when I struck. With his guard down, I stepped forward and flicked a right jab that caught him just above the eye. I pounded him with a hard left to the chin, then popped him with a right to the nose. O'Shea's snot locker made a crunching sound, and blood began to flow. The blows stunned him, and he stumbled backward. The crowd noise increased as I went after the bully. Once he gathered himself, our combat became more defensive.

"Time!" called the lieutenant.

We returned to our sides of the circle. During the break between rounds, I watched Mike carefully. His breathing was deep and heavy. Though several cuts had opened on his face, he had a determined, angry look. Pick massaged my shoulders. "Jarek, you can't street-fight Mike. If you keep boxing like your father taught you, you can take him. Keep moving and look for your spots. When you caught him on the nose in that last round, he was stunned. Circle to your left and sting him again."

"Box!"

Mike charged across the ring. I slipped to the side and delivered some hard shots to his ribs. He quickly covered, protecting his midsection with his elbows. He lashed out with a right. I ducked beneath the punch and delivered an uppercut, driving my right hand into his stomach. He grunted, and dropped his guard a bit lower. My gloves then went to his face. I was working the fight like Father had taught me.

I moved in closer, planning to pop him on the chin, when a powerful left hand caught me on the side of the head. My ears started ringing and I staggered to the side. Mike closed in as I shook my head to get rid of the cobwebs.

"Move, Jarek! Move!" someone shouted.

Through my blurred vision, I saw a few guys in the circle

holding up clenched fists throwing punches in the air. I was trying to fight back, but my arms felt like rubber. I collected myself and fended off a hard right with my gloves. Then I tagged Mike with a left to the chin that stood him up straight. The crowd was on its toes, shouting and cheering the action.

Mike and I circled each other, issuing fake punches and moving cautiously. He moved in and I side-stepped to the left. From out of nowhere, Mike delivered a crushing blow that found its way between my gloves, catching me square on the chin. Everything went fuzzy. I dropped to my knees as he kept up a flurry of blows. The crowd shouted for me to get up. I couldn't find my legs.

The lieutenant stepped in, "Break it up! Break it up!"

It was over, but nothing was over. I hoped my fight with Mike O'Shea would solve things. I was wrong. Mike would certainly gloat over his victory. He wouldn't forget my challenge. It appeared as though our fight only made matters worse, and nothing would bring Squint back. Nothing!

Before breakfast, I put a cold washcloth on my eye and washed the blood off my face. After morning inspection, I headed to the tool shed to pick up my shovel, as I had every day since my first days at camp. The lieutenant stopped me.

"Sokolowski," he said, calling me aside. "Captain wants to see you now."

A thousand questions raced through my mind. Above all, I was worried about keeping my job. If I were to be kicked out of the CCC, it would be another cruel blow to my family. Each step toward the captain's office added worry and dread.

Why did the captain want to see me?

TWENTY-SEVEN

Officers' Quarters

THE OFFICERS' QUARTERS WAS A SEPARATE BUILDING TUCKED away near the mess hall and opposite the rec hall. I straightened myself before knocking on the door.

"Come in."

The captain sat behind a large oak desk facing away from me. He was bent over in his chair, studying the contents of a file folder.

"Take a seat, Sokolowski," the captain said matter-of-factly.

As I sat, I studied the room. Plaques and citations lined the walls. All were hung straight and true. Papers on the captain's desktop were square to the corners and neatly stacked. The room smelled of disinfectant, not altogether unpleasant, but sterile and strong.

Captain Mason continued to give his attention to the file folder. The silence was uncomfortable. My guts churned with worry. Had my fight with Mike been the cause of this meeting? Was my offense so great that I had put my family on the spot? I'd seen other enrollees discharged for a variety of offenses. My knees started knocking, and I broke out in a sweat.

I couldn't take the silence any longer. "You asked to see me, sir?"

The captain raised an index finger to quiet me. Then he pulled his hand back and adjusted his reading glasses. The silence continued. Each minute felt like an hour.

Finally the captain swiveled. He carefully removed his glasses, folding and placing them square to the edge of his desk. "Sokolowski, we have serious matters to discuss."

A hard knot formed in the pit of my stomach. I sat up straight and alert. If it was to be bad news, I would face it without blinking. I would face it like a man.

"First off," the captain began, "I'm sorry to learn about the loss of your brother. I wish to extend my most sincere sympathies."

His comment took me totally off guard. I opened my mouth, but no sounds came out.

He cleared his throat with a *harrumph* before continuing. "I don't know what it's like to lose a brother ... never had one. But I have lost people close to me. If you need to take off a few days—with pay, of course—I will grant permission for a furlough."

I was surprised by his understanding and his gesture of

kindness. The captain had always seemed so distant. This was a side of him I'd never seen.

"Thank you, sir, but I'd like to stay on the job, if it's all the same to you."

The captain nodded. The wisp of a smile crossed his face. "Very well, Sokolowski."

"Is that all, sir?" I asked as I put my hands on my knees and prepared to stand.

"No, that is not all," the captain waved, motioning for me to remain seated. He raised the manila folder he was studying when I arrived. "You're taking a class in motor vehicle operation, is that correct?"

"Yes, sir. I want to be a truck driver. It's all I've ever wanted to do." The course of our conversation was taking a direction that confused and excited me. "If you need truck drivers, I'm sure I'd do a dandy job for you."

Without taking his eyes off the folder, the captain responded crisply. "No, you will not be a truck driver, Sokolowski. I'm promoting you to assistant leader."

"What?" I asked in genuine surprise. "Why?"

The captain focused his eyes on me. "You don't know, do you?"

I shook my head in dumb disbelief.

"Have you noticed that other enrollees follow you? They trust you to do what is right. You're a natural leader." The captain leaned in toward me. "Just the other day, you took charge of a group of enrollees, leading them out of harm's way when the wildfire crowned. Without your leadership and judgment, lives would have been lost."

Captain Mason stood up and walked around his desk, leaning on a corner. "You took control in a desperate situation. Not everybody does that." He paused before continuing. "Think back to when your buddy went AWOL. When you came directly to me, you were taking a risk. You knew that you were breaking the chain of command by going around Assistant Leader O'Shea. Still, you were doing what you thought was right. You stood up for Campeau. That shows courage and initiative."

The captain put his hand on my shoulder and looked me square in the eye. "The boys in camp respect you. Everybody knows that you've taken a lot of grief from Assistant Leader O'Shea." The captain gave a wry little smile. "I'll bet that someone close to you was responsible for the skunk that ended up in his tent."

I let out a laugh, giving away the secret.

He turned serious. "Sokolowski, the enrollees at Polack Lake look up to you. Most would like to be a part of your team." He paused for a moment. "You're a bear hunter. I need people who show backbone, take initiative, and are natural leaders."

I was bewildered by what the captain was saying.

"People like Assistant Leader O'Shea are bullies and blowhards. They get things done by pushing and browbeating. People like him are needed in the CCC, but they're a dime a dozen. You, Sokolowski, are very different."

I was speechless. When I first entered the captain's office, my mind was full of worry about getting booted out of the CCC. Now I was worried about the burden of a new responsibility.

"As of this month, Sokolowski, you'll be receiving an additional $6 in your pay."

The thought of $6 more each month was overwhelming. "Will the CCC send the extra money to my family?"

"The money is yours. Do with it what you will."

"Thank you, sir!" I stood and extended my hand. His handshake was firm and sincere.

"You're welcome," the captain said before shifting his gaze to his desk. "You may be thanking me now, but being a leader can be tough duty. Getting enrollees to do things they don't want to do will take all of your skills. So, before starting your new job, I'm ordering you to take the rest of the day off. Put a cold washcloth on your face. It'll help keep the swelling down."

As I turned to leave, the captain offered one more comment. "Oh, Sokolowski, there's a staff meeting in the mess hall at 7:00 this evening. Please be on time."

TWENTY-EIGHT

Time to Think

I DIDN'T ARGUE WITH CAPTAIN MASON WHEN HE TOLD ME TO take the day off. After applying a cold compress to my face, I decided to take a long walk. Most of my time at Polack Lake had been spent either at the camp or in the pit. A nice walk was exactly what I needed to clear my head. I headed east to get away from the fire area and most of the work activity. On the way out of camp, the crest of a low ridge gave me a commanding view of our community in the wilderness. I marveled at just how much had been accomplished in a short time by a pack of skinny cats.

Dust kicked up from my heels as I continued down the two-track road. Dirty gray sand crept into my shoes. I stopped by the side of the trail to empty them out. For a while, I walked barefoot, feeling the grit between my toes.

The smell of summer was heavy on the air. The few remaining trees were in their full majesty. Insects buzzed and swooped. The wildflowers were in bloom, and blackberries offered a treat for the eyes and the tongue.

Somehow, I found myself at the edge of a clearing. A tall oak that had not been taken by the lumber companies stood proudly to one side. Its stout branches were like arms welcoming a weary traveler. It had been a long time since I'd climbed a tree. The wind in the leaves whispered an invitation that couldn't be ignored. I dropped my shoes and took hold of a branch that hovered above my head. My feet grabbed at the rough bark, toes helping to secure the grip. Higher and higher I climbed, until I found a resting place.

Two branches that had sprouted closely together formed an easy chair that was just my size. I took a restful seat there overlooking the clearing. The gentle wind moved blades of grass and leaves in nearby trees. One seemed to call. The other would respond in kind. It was nature's dance. Black-capped chickadees, pine sparrows, blue jays, and other northland birds squeaked and squawked noisily.

A sudden movement caught my attention. A couple of fox pups were playing nearby. They tumbled in the tall grass, nipping at each other's ears. The pups took turns chasing. Back and forth they played. They made me think of Squint and how we would rough and tumble. Despite the yelping and pawing, the love between brothers was something very special. I enjoyed watching their games, but I couldn't control the flow of tears.

Back at camp, word got around quickly about my

promotion to assistant leader. By the time I showed up at the staff meeting, I had been congratulated by nearly everyone. The only notable exception was Mike O'Shea. He was the last to show up at the meeting. Mike's appearance was shocking. He had two black eyes that made him look like a raccoon. His lower lip was fat and bore a wide split. It was apparent that Big Mike got every bit as much as he gave.

Lieutenant Campbell formally introduced me as the newest assistant leader at Camp Polack Lake, and the staff applauded—except for Mike. As the meeting progressed, updates were offered on various projects and activities. Roads and trails continued to be cut through the Marquette National Forest. Miles of additional telephone cable were being strung.

Mr. Wilson reported on clean-up operations that had been taking place in the area of the wildfire. A team of enrollees had been going back to the site each day. They carried heavy backpack sprayers filled with water to douse hot spots and put out small outbreaks that flared up from time to time. The forester indicated that it would take a while to get everything under control. At the end of his report, he commented that the enrollees on mop-up duty were getting tired and that their fatigue could prolong the work.

One of the experienced local men reported on the progress of a surveying team he was leading. The enrollees were doing a good job of learning how to operate the equipment. Soon they would be ready to work on their own. Another local man reported on the construction of a third fire tower north of camp.

Mike glared at me through the entire meeting. Once the reports were over, Lieutenant Campbell stood. "Any questions or comments?"

I stood so everyone could hear me. "I know I'm the new guy here, but ever since coming to Polack Lake, I've been working with a crew in the gravel pit. The scenery never changes down there." Several of the leaders chuckled. "I think the guys in the pit would like to see something different. I'd like to volunteer my team to trade places with the mop-up crew."

"Is that all right with you, Mr. Wilson?" the lieutenant asked.

"Heck, yes," said the forester. "Have your enrollees meet me after breakfast tomorrow. The boys on my mop-up crew will report to Mr. O'Shea."

The meeting was adjourned, and I headed back to the barracks. Mike hung back to meet me in the shadows. "It ain't over between you and me."

I stopped and faced him. "Yes, it is. Fighting with you didn't solve anything. It never will." I turned sharply and walked away.

I smiled as I crossed the parade grounds. Trading jobs with the mop-up crew was a stroke of genius. Not only would we get out of the pit, we'd be out from under Mike's thumb.

My smile wouldn't last long.

TWENTY-NINE

Out of the Frying Pan

August 1934

MR. WILSON PULLED THE SUPPLY TRUCK INTO THE CAMPSITE right after breakfast. My work crew joined him just as he was opening a map of the burned-out area we left only days before. He had completed an inspection tour earlier in the morning. On the map he located hot spots that needed attention. We were issued fire rakes, axes, and shovels. We were also introduced to the sprayers. After some basic instructions, we loaded up on the truck and began wheeling toward new scenery and away from the pit.

Some ideas sound better than they really are. If the pit was bad, mop-up operations were awful. It didn't take long for the griping to begin. The work was dirty and difficult. The ground was still hot in places. The stale stink of burned-out wilderness soiled our noses. Ash covered everything, including us, with a powdery coating of grit. Each stroke of the rake, strike of the axe, or push of the shovel raised a cloud that floated on the air—only to be taken in by our lungs. Handkerchiefs couldn't begin to filter it. Dry ash and dust had a bitter taste. It settled in our ears and stung our eyes. We coughed and choked violently as we worked.

Yasku removed the dirty handkerchief from his face to wipe the sweat from his forehead. He leaned on his shovel and focused his gaze on me. From his nose on up, his face was black with soot; from his nose on down, it was pale white. "So, you *volunteered* us for this duty?"

I cast my eyes down. "I was trying to help."

"Well, thanks for nothing." Yasku spit soot out of his mouth. Then he replaced his handkerchief and slowly returned to the task of spreading embers from a hot spot. "At least in the pit we didn't have to put up with this heat, stench, and dirt," Yasku muttered without looking at me.

Pick struggled with the heavy sprayer and laid a swath of water over some hot embers. They hissed and sputtered. Through the handkerchief, Pick muttered, "Don't do us no more favors, Jarek."

During the lunch break, I went to join the guys. One by one, they left, forming their own circle. Mr. Wilson came to join me, easing himself against the back of his truck. He removed a straight-stemmed pipe from his pocket, cleaned the soot off, and stuffed it with tobacco. His eyes scanned the sky as he struck a match and drew on the pipe.

"Ain't easy being an assistant leader, is it?" Mr. Wilson said as he let a puff of smoke escape the side of his mouth.

"I don't understand it," I said. "Last night the guys were

all slapping me on the back, congratulating me. Today, all they want to do is gripe." I scratched my head and soot wafted from my hair. "Looks like I made a mistake volunteering for mop-up detail."

"Maybe, maybe not," Mr. Wilson said as he tamped the tobacco down in his pipe and relit. A small cloud of smoke encircled his head. "It's human nature for people to rebel against authority, especially new authority. People just love to test limits."

"But these fellas are my friends," I said.

Mr. Wilson put his pipe down by his side, crossed his legs and looked me in the eye. "Sokolowski, you ain't being paid to be a friend. You're being paid to be an assistant leader. So, act like one."

"What do you mean?"

"Go toe-to-toe with these guys and stop the griping—the sooner the better. Let them know who's in charge, and that you won't put up with their carping." He took a long, slow draw off his pipe and released the smoke before continuing. "You don't have to be mean or cruel, but you've got to lay down the law."

He left me to think. I knew he was right. I needed to show some backbone. Five minutes before lunch break was over, I took action. "Gather up," I shouted. The guys grumbled and slowly got to their feet. "Double-time over here or you'll all be pulling KP tonight." The team quickstepped over to where I was standing.

"What's with you?" Stosh asked. The others muttered in agreement.

"You've made it clear that you aren't happy with your

new work assignment. Well, I've got news for you: this fire needs to be put down for good and we're the ones who are going to do it. If you don't like it, just say the word. There's a train leaving from town that runs back down to the Lower Peninsula every day."

I let my words sink in before continuing. "From now on, I don't want to hear your griping. Give me a fair day's work, and we'll get along. Now, get to work."

The fellas grumbled in low whispers, but not to me. Still, they kept up the work and did a good job. After getting back to camp that afternoon, I moved my bunk to one of the other barracks. Fortunately, I found a place to stay that didn't house my friends or Mike O'Shea. It wasn't easy to leave my buddies, but I felt that it was something that had to be done.

At supper I sat with some of the boys from my new barrack. Out of the corner of my eye, I watched my friends from Grand Rapids across the room. From time to time they looked in my direction and talked amongst themselves. It was hard to keep my distance.

The captain and Mr. Wilson were right: being a leader wasn't all that it was cracked up to be.

THIRTY

Distant Thunder

WEEKS AFTER I WAS PROMOTED TO ASSISTANT LEADER, I HAD
my last class in motor vehicle operations. Each student
took turns driving a gravel truck. One of the guys from my
new barrack came close to backing over the flagpole in the
parade grounds. We all earned certificates for successfully
completing the class. Afterwards, I walked to the rec hall to
write a letter to Sophia.

In one part of the building, some enrollees were playing
cards. A ping-pong game was going on in another area. I took
a table near the book shelves and settled down to write. My
world had changed completely in recent days. How would I
share all that happened?

I wanted to tell my family how I felt about losing Squint,
my fight with Mike, and my promotion to assistant leader.

As I worked through my message, I never felt more alone in my life. Along with all that happened to me, my new job forced me to separate from the friends who had been by my side since I was a kid. I wrote and rewrote my letter home. The wastebasket near me filled to the brim with discarded letters.

Father had been right when he said that "for a boy to become a man is very hard." The highlight of my letter home was to announce that I would be sending them an extra $6 a month. The money would make life just a bit easier for them. Still nothing would ease the grief of losing Squint. I wasn't totally happy with the letter, but I dropped it in the mail slot just the same. The right words did not exist.

It was a hot, muggy night as I slipped into the sack before lights-out. The cicadas played a symphony of rhythmic chirping sounds. Bullfrogs were croaking their nighttime chorus and mosquitoes buzzed. Off in the distance, thunder rolled like giant drums. My eyes were wide open, staring at the ceiling through the dark of night. So very much had happened, and I was operating in new territory.

It felt like I hadn't fallen asleep at all when the whistle blew and the call came for everyone to assemble. It was just after 3:00 a.m. "Off and on! Off and on! Off your backs and on your feet!" someone shouted from the parade grounds. My feet hit the floor, and I jumped into my clothes.

I knew what it was the minute I stepped out of my barrack. The horizon off to the northwest was aglow. The telltale odor of smoke floated on the wind. Enrollees began pouring out of their barracks as Mr. Wilson pulled his truck to a stop right in front of me. A cloud of dust from his wheels covered me. "Can you drive?" he asked.

"Sure. I just passed motor vehicle operations."

"Then drive." Mr. Wilson climbed into the passenger side as I took the wheel.

"Where are we going?"

Mr. Wilson looked at me like I had a hole in my head. Then he pointed toward the glow on the horizon. "That way, boy," he said, "go that way."

I popped the clutch and the truck started with a neck-snapping jerk. Headlights bounced off the road ahead, turning curious animal eyes into reflectors. As I drove, Mr. Wilson studied his map by the dim glow of a flashlight. We were several miles out of camp when he first spoke. "We're looking for the best place to fight this fire. If we can find a natural break, like a road or a river that's in its path, we'll draw the line there."

As we pushed toward the fire, the countryside choked with clouds of drifting smoke. Hot ash tinged with glowing edges wafted down from the sky like fiery snow. Wind from the southwest was driving the beast toward us.

"Stop!" Mr. Wilson shouted.

I jammed on the brakes and the truck swerved hard to the right. Mr. Wilson jumped out and climbed a high ridge next to the road. He carefully scanned the area with his binoculars before scrambling back to the vehicle. I held the flashlight for him as he manipulated the compass and looked at his old map.

"There's a railroad track that runs just north of here,"

said Mr. Wilson. "That's where we'll make our stand. Now, let's get out of here before we're cooked alive."

I spun the truck around on the narrow road and headed back to camp as fast as I could. There was no time to waste. The countryside was as dry as a bone, and this fire was moving fast.

THIRTY-ONE

Fighting the Beast

MR. WILSON BRIEFED ALL THE LEADERS AND ASSISTANT LEADERS on the size and movement of the fire. His worn, crumpled map was spread out on a table so we could all see it clearly. He used a pen as a pointer to show where the fire was, the direction of its path, and the railroad bed that would be our line of defense. Assignments and working orders were given sharply. Within minutes, the trucks were loaded and two hundred young gladiators armed with hand tools were on their way to face the beast. Bulldozers and tractors with huge V-plows would also join the fight.

I took my place in the cab of the lead vehicle with Mr. Wilson behind the wheel. My team and Mike and his team rode in the back. As we approached the edge of the fire, Mr. Wilson turned north on a seldom-used two-rut trail.

Low-hanging branches slapped at the windshield, and brush screeched and scraped at the side of the truck. After a few miles of twisting and turning trail, we found the railroad bed. Mr. Wilson stopped and ran back to the other drivers in the caravan, giving them their final instructions. Smoke was beginning to pour across the tracks.

When he got back, he raced the engine and drove down the railroad bed. At regular intervals he signaled trailing vehicles. They dropped off enrollees and equipment. When the boys hit the ground, they started working, extending the natural fire break that the railroad tracks offered.

We were the last to be dropped off—the end of the fire line. Mike and his team were just to the east of us. Fire rakes, axes, and shovels immediately went to work. Heavy smoke didn't start rolling in until a half hour later. Our pace quickened. Soon the wind pushed burning leaves and embers in our direction. Mike screamed orders to his team. We were all working as hard and as fast as we could. The forest was being pushed back inch by inch, foot by foot. We prayed it would be enough to stop the beast.

Mr. Wilson left his truck off to the west, hoping that it would be out of the fire's reach. He jogged along the track to inspect the work. Another part of his job was to direct the setup of portable wells and pumps. He left the tracks and went deep into the brush. Now and then we could hear him calling out directions to the pump crews.

Much of the Upper Peninsula is swampy and low. In many areas, water lays just a few feet below the surface. Shallow wells could be dug in a matter of minutes. Three shallow wells were sunk to support the fight. These wells were strategically located downwind from the fire and several hundred feet behind the skirmish line. Gas-operated pumps drew water from the wells. Thick hoses ran from the well sites to the fire line. CCC boys were assigned to concentrate the flow of water on hot spots. The simple gas engines chugged as they worked. The water they supplied would be poured on the fire in an attempt to quench a monster that is forever thirsty. The pumps were a firefighting tool that hadn't been available to us in our first fire fight.

The clank and clatter of tools rang through the early morning hours. The handkerchiefs over our faces blocked the flying ash from getting into our lungs. Still, we coughed as we inhaled the stinging smoke. Steadily, the noise we were making was overtaken by the roar of the fire. Flames emerged from the south. Heat waves licked at us and took away our energy. Hot cinders flew around, burning holes in our clothes. The hair on our heads and arms that had just grown back since the last fire was being singed off once again.

The tamarack and cedar trees in the area of the fire fed the creature, cracking and popping as they were swallowed. The intensity of the heat was overwhelming, forcing the work crews farther back from the railroad bed. Our firefighting went from offensively building a wider fire break to defensively fighting outbreaks of flames that had jumped the railroad bed. The beast coughed up sparks and embers that danced on the air like fireflies. We struggled to beat out the flames that were trying to establish themselves. Pumps worked furiously, wetting down the dry timber and dousing flames that tried to gain purchase on our side of the break.

Nearby, a bulldozer emerged from the haze of smoke and waves of heat. The man driving the dozer held his arm at eye level to shield his face. Trees and brush fell to the blade, giving a wider margin of safety to the break. We cheered as the machine headed toward us. The chug of the engine was barely audible over the roar of the beast. Suddenly, the dozer bogged down, then ground to a halt. The man hopped off, grabbed a fire rake, and joined us in the fight.

The battle with the beast was pitched. When the fire moved forward, we struggled to beat it back. We would gain ground, and then the fire would advance. The creature was persistent, testing weaknesses in the line and challenging our spirit. Streams of water were our best defense in the struggle; they also cooled us from the waves of heat that swept across the fire line.

Just when it looked like we were gaining the upper hand, the sharp sound of an explosion shot through the early morning darkness. The stream of water that was our lifeline began to wither, then fell to nothing. We had lost our pump. The fire surged across the break a quarter-mile to the east. Mike and one of the other assistant leaders moved their crews to fight the advance.

No one had any idea of the horror that was unfolding.

THIRTY-TWO

Surrounded

DESPERATE SHOUTS CAME FROM THE AREA OF THE OUTBREAK. The dozer was down, and the water pump was out of commission after the explosion. Worse yet, gasoline from the exploding pump set a second fire behind us. On all fronts, the beast was edging forward with growing confidence. We were losing our battle. We were fast becoming surrounded. To our west, between us and Mr. Wilson's truck, the fire extended an ugly claw.

I moved my team to face the new outbreak to the west. The wind whipped as we pushed against the fire. Flames hopped across the railroad bed, driving the fire deeper into the forest. "It's going to trap us!" I shouted as the beast grew around us in nearly every direction. "Get out before we're surrounded!"

The boys followed as I ran between torches of fire and blazing timber. Flames licked at bare arms, singeing hair and eyebrows. I emerged on the other side of the outbreak and began counting heads as they followed behind me. There were two missing, one was Pick. I edged as close to the flames as I could, shouting his name. From the far side of the fiery wall I heard screams for help. The arms of the beast were growing stronger, gathering its prey and preparing for the kill.

I turned to my team. Faces were cast in horror. "Look for a gap in the fire," I shouted. "Maybe there's a way to get them out." Stosh picked two boys to go with him. The group wove their way through tangles and trees, paralleling the path of the fire. The rest of the team paced and fretted, worrying about the lives of their friends. As I looked for answers, a thought came to me. I suddenly knew what had to be done.

"Get off the railroad bed," I ordered. The boys moved away from the direction of the fire and off into the nearby woods while I headed for Mr. Wilson's truck. There were two sprayers and a pile of blankets in the back. I hoped it would be enough to do the job. If I could break through, it might just work.

I slid behind the wheel and closed the door solidly. The engine growled as I shifted into gear. Gravel flew from under the tires, tapping loudly against the metal frame. The truck gathered speed as I steered as close to the tracks as I could. My eyes focused dead ahead, hands gripping the wheel tightly. The wall of fire got closer, closer. I jumped on the accelerator, pounding the pedal to the floor.

Heat and fire encircled the truck as I drove through the wall. When the truck entered the flames, I began counting out loud to time how long it would take to break through. Within a four-count, I was on the other side and laying on the horn. Pick and another fella appeared from the smoky haze, stumbling as they ran for the safety of the vehicle. I opened the door to hail them.

"Get in the back!" I shouted at the top of my lungs. "Wet down the blankets with the sprayers, but don't use all the water."

I rolled the truck down the rail bed a few hundred feet. The truck's horn was muffled by the sound of wildfire. Twelve more stragglers were eventually loaded on board. I ordered Pick to look the truck over for damage. He quickly ran around it. One of the tires was beginning to smolder, so he doused it with a few shots of water from the sprayer.

"Runnin' low on water!" Pick hollered as he tossed the sprayer into the back of the truck.

Towering ahead of us was another wall of flame, larger and more violent than the first. It was time to get out. As I began to turn the vehicle around, someone beat on the top of the cab. I opened the door.

"A few more are trapped on the other side!" he shouted, pointing to the giant flames ahead. "One of 'em is Mike."

I swallowed hard. There was no question about what had to be done. "Everybody out!" I ordered. "Take a few wet blankets, cover yourselves, and stay together. I'll be right back." Once again, I pointed the truck down the bed of the tracks.

The truck tossed and heaved as it penetrated the thick

skin of the beast. This time it took a ten-count before emerging through the far side. I gave the horn a long blast, and then climbed out to inspect for damage. The lives of many CCC boys, including mine, relied on this beat-up old truck. The tires were smoking, but sound. I emptied one of the sprayers putting out a few spots in the truck bed, then tossed it aside before climbing back aboard.

The heat was overwhelming, and the fire was growing more intense by the minute. I hit the horn a few more times. If I was to save those behind me, I couldn't stay much longer. Other boys were supposed to be here, but I couldn't see anyone.

With only moments to spare, I ran into the woods, calling out for survivors. Just as I was about to give up, ghostly figures appeared ahead of me. They were silhouetted against the red and orange of the flames. The beast was consuming the brush and fallen timber all around them.

I ran up to them and saw that they were struggling to move a fallen tree. Someone was pinned underneath it. It was Mike O'Shea. The tree was pressing down hard on his chest.

"What do we do?" one of the guys shouted above the roar of the fire. "Mike was cutting down this tree, and it fell on him. We can't move it!"

Mike struggled to speak. His words came out in a painful whisper. We had to lean down close in order to hear him. "Leave me. Save yourselves."

I cupped my hands around my mouth and spoke loudly so the two boys could hear clearly. "We're not leaving him here to die. Find something sturdy that we can use as a lever."

One of the boys spotted a thick branch on the ground nearby. We slid part of it under the tree next to Mike's chest and took a solid grip. The three of us began to lift. Our backs strained. The branch cracked under the pressure. Slowly, the tree inched upward. While the two others struggled to keep the tree off Mike, I took hold of his arms and pulled.

Somehow, some way, the plan worked. When the pressure was off his chest, Mike gasped deeply, taking hot air into his lungs. He was badly burned and coughed uncontrollably. There was no time, and this was no place to give him first aid. We quickly gathered him up and helped him back to the truck.

As I climbed up into the battered vehicle, I shouted, "Cover up with the blankets back there. I'll get you out of here."

THIRTY-THREE

Conquering the Beast

I CROSSED MYSELF AND MUTTERED A QUICK PRAYER. GETTING to this point was not easy. Getting out with everyone alive would be more difficult.

The truck started up like a champ. I gave the dashboard a loving pat. But, when I went to shift it into gear, there was nothing. I moved the stick, trying to coax the transmission to life. It wouldn't move out of neutral. I tried again—nothing! Desperately I worked the shift lever, searching blindly for first gear—nothing! I turned off the engine and popped the hood on the truck, praying for a quick and easy fix.

The shift mechanism traveled down into the bowels of the machine. A piece of tree limb was stuck in the middle of the linkage, jamming the gear shift. Desperate, I found a rock and started beating on the wood—once, twice, three times—until I heard a loud pop. I didn't know if what I had done would work, but there was no more time. The beast was crowding in from all sides. I slammed the hood down.

"Get us out of here!" someone in the back shouted.

I didn't take the time to answer. Instead, I turned the key in the ignition again. The truck started. I slammed it into gear. This time it made the heavenly grinding sound of a transmission engaged. The vehicle spun around, tossing gravel as we headed back toward the flames. It was the only way out.

Halfway through the wall, I heard a loud bang. The truck swerved hard to the right. I fought to keep it straight. Emerging through the far side, I stopped in front of the waiting survivors, leaving the engine running. "Check for damage," I shouted to no one in particular. "There's a sprayer back there that has a little water in it."

Someone jumped into the bed of the truck and grabbed the remaining sprayer while the others hopped on board. "You've got a blow-out," he shouted, "left rear. Everything else looks okay."

"Spray down the blankets with what water there is left, and make sure everybody's covered up."

My heart pounded. Sweat poured down my brow. There was one more wall of fire to negotiate. The truck had to hold together. I had to hold together. My leg shook as I eased out the clutch. The old truck came to life slowly. It gathered speed grudgingly. "Ka-lunk, ka-lunk" the flat tire slapped against the frame of the vehicle. My knuckles were white and sore from gripping the wheel so tightly. I winced as the truck entered the hellish wall of fire.

Ten-count ... twelve-count ... fourteen-count ... at long last we were through. Clean air had never felt so good! Morning sunshine washed over us. The truck ground to a halt, and I slumped behind the wheel. Two more tires blew and the vehicle slowly sank beneath me. It took a while before I could release my fingers from the steering wheel and climb down out of the cab. My knees shook as everyone cheered and jumped for joy, circling me and pounding me on the back.

"Is everybody okay?" I asked.

"Mike's burned pretty bad," someone called from the back of the truck.

"Get him out of there!" I ordered. The boys used a blanket as a makeshift stretcher and gently hauled him down. They laid him on the soft grass beside the railroad bed. Mike's hair was singed down to the scalp. His face was blistered with burns and his eyes looked like slits in swollen skin.

"Get the first-aid kit out of the truck," I said. "Somebody give him some water."

As others treated his burns, I knelt beside him. "It's over, Mike. You're safe now."

Tears formed in the corners of his eyes. His lips moved slightly as he tried to speak, but no words came. He lifted a hand and gripped me firmly on my forearm.

"I know, Mike," I said, choking back tears of my own. "I know. You rest now."

The fire was eventually put out by the CCC. Through the

fight, they demonstrated bravery, courage, and determination. That day in the wilderness, all the CCC boys earned the right to be called men.

What's more, the most terrible of all beasts had been conquered.

Epilogue

IN JULY OF 1936, TEN BOYS OF CCC COMPANY 686 WERE trapped in the DuFour Creek fire, a blaze that consumed 923 acres of Michigan forest land. An enrollee truck driver named Walter Stokes drove along a railroad bed and through walls of flame in order to save his stranded friends. All were rescued, and Walter Stokes was honored for valor.

During only the first enrollment period of the Civilian Conservation Corps in Michigan—April 1 to October 1, 1933—enrollees constructed 67 miles of fire breaks, 556 miles of fire trails, and 543 acres that were used primarily as landing fields for observation airplanes. They also gave 32,807 man-days to the task of fighting wildfires.

(Source: *We Can Do It! A History of the CCC in Michigan, 1933–1942* by Charles A. Symon, 1983)

Glossary

Following is a glossary of terms from the Depression, the CCC, and the Polish language:

AWOL: Absent without leave, a military term

Backfire: 1) A fire that is intentionally lit to prevent a wildfire from spreading, or 2) An explosion that comes from an engine, usually when starting, stopping or accelerating

Beat the daylights: Knock someone unconscious, as in a fight

Bone to pick: An argument or disagreement

***Brat*:** Brother (Polish)

Bunk: 1) Bed, or 2) An expression of disbelief

Button: Nose

Clean your clock: Beat someone in a fight

Cookie: Camp cook

Dime a dozen: Cheap, easy to find

Dole: Public assistance from the government

Drip torches: Torches that, when lit, would drip burning material to intentionally start a line of fire

Dukes: Fists, as in "put up your dukes," an invitation to fight

Eight ball: 1) A game played on a pool table, or 2) Someone who is a misfit

Feeling his oats: Feeling better, stronger

Furlough: Military term for time off or vacation

Goldbrick: Lazy, someone who avoids work

Grub hoe: A two-headed tool used for digging; one end is a pick and the opposite end is a six-inch wide blade

Heebie-jeebies: Nervous, the jitters

Hit the sack: Go to bed

Hobo jungle: An area where homeless people or vagrants gather

Hobo: Homeless person or vagrant

***Kolega*:** Friend (Polish)

KP: Kitchen Police; military term for kitchen or clean-up detail, usually as a form of punishment

LEM: Local Experienced Men; men hired by the CCC to supervise work and to teach work skills to enrollees

Local experienced men: (See LEM)

***Matka*:** Mother (Polish)

Maw: Mouth

Mess hall or tent: Dining room

Mess kit: A compact kit of metal pots, pans, and plates that is used by soldiers and campers for cooking and serving food

Mud: Coffee

Ojciec: Father (Polish)

Palooka: Inexperienced or incompetent

Railroad bull: Security guard hired by the railroad company

Rodzina: Family (Polish)

Rub: Conflict between people

Rube: A hick, someone who is ignorant

Sack: Bed

Shuteye: Sleep

Siostra: Sister (Polish)

Snitch: Steal

Snot locker: Nose

Starszy: Older (Polish)

Stirring up a hornet's nest: Creating more problems

Toe-to-toe: Get in someone's face, look someone in the eye

Turned tail: Run away, usually scared

Two bits: A quarter of a dollar, 25 cents

Waiting on pins and needles: Waiting nervously

Author's Notes

1. **Historical Fiction**—*Fires in the Wilderness* is a story of fictional characters placed in an historical setting. Often authors of historical fiction take some liberties with history. However, they try to keep true to the times and circumstances. The characters in this story are the creations of the author. However, an individual nicknamed "Squint" did enroll in the CCC and did wash out at Camp Custer. Many of the events in this story are built on recollections of men who were once CCC boys. Can you think of an historical event that would be fun to write a fictional story about?

2. **Simile**—Similes and metaphors are tools that writers use to help readers gain a deeper understanding of feelings and circumstances. A simile is a figure of speech

that compares things that are typically unlike each other. Similes follow phrases that start with the words *like* or *as*. In Chapter 1, "Skinny Cats," of this book, the main character says: "I felt *like* one of those skinny cats."

3. **Metaphors** are figures of speech in which a word or phrase that ordinarily means one thing is used as a comparison for something else. Metaphors do not use the words *like* or *as*. Later on in Chapter 1, you can find the sentence: "We were skinny cats running for our lives." This can be viewed as a metaphor. How would you describe your life as a simile or a metaphor?

4. **Foreshadowing** is a device that writers use to give the reader a clue about what will happen later in the story. In the second chapter of *Fires in the Wilderness*, Jarek has a dream that gives a clue into the future. What does this dream describe? Can Jarek's father's advice in the first chapter also be considered foreshadowing?

5. **Protagonist and Antagonist**—A protagonist is typically the main character of a story. The protagonist in *Fires in the Wilderness* is Jarek Sokolowski. An antagonist is someone or something opposing the protagonist. The antagonist in *Fires in the Wilderness* is introduced in Chapter 2, "Train to Tomorrow:" Can you identify the antagonist?

6. **Character Development**—Authors develop the primary characters (protagonist and antagonist) to help readers understand them, and give some feeling for the

supporting characters. How is Jarek like his friends? How is he different? What kind of person is Captain Mason? What about Ben, who shared the umbrella tent with the Polish friends?

7. **Bullying and Discrimination as a Basis for Conflict**—Bullying is a form of harassment by someone who has more physical and/or social power and dominance than the victim. In *Fires in the Wilderness*, Mike O'Shea is the antagonist and a bully. Through the course of the story, he harasses Jarek because of his nationality. This creates the story's conflict. What other forms of discrimination exist? An excellent research project would be to do a report on how African-Americans and Native Americans were treated by the CCC.

8. **History Lesson**—Camp Custer still exists in Battle Creek, Michigan. The military camp was named after General George Armstrong Custer. One history challenge is to learn why a military camp in Michigan came to be named after General Custer.

9. **Depression Cash**—CCC enrollees earned $30 a month. Of that amount, $25 was sent home. That doesn't seem like much money today. According to calculations using the Consumer Price Index, the purchasing power of $1 in 1933 was worth $15.56 in 2006. How much would $25 dollars in 1933 be worth in 2006?

10. **Personal History:** In Chapter 7, "Training," Jarek Sokolowski was issued serial number CC6-104377. This

was the actual serial number of the author's father, who served in the Civilian Conservation Corps in 1935, at Camp Cusino in Michigan's Upper Peninsula. Family history is often the source of inspiration for authors. Write a paragraph about someone in your family history who did or was involved in something that is of interest to you.

11. **Humor** is an essential part of life. Through the course of *Fires in the Wilderness*, the friends have fun with each other, and even play a practical joke on the antagonist. What is your favorite humorous event in the story?

12. **Word Choice**—The military has a special language. Terms that one group develops that aren't understood by another group are referred to as *jargon*. The author chose several military terms that were used in the CCC: mess kit, mess tent, KP, AWOL, and others. In addition, *jargon* and phrases from the Depression era were also used: railroad bull, LaSalle (automobile), and rube, among others. You probably use words that are unfamiliar to your parents or grandparents. Make a list of those words—your jargon.

13. **Idioms**—An idiom is a combination of words whose meaning is different from the individual words themselves. Each generation and group (such as the military) have their own idioms. In the first chapter of *Fires in the Wilderness*, Pick says, "Hold your horses." By saying this, Pick isn't asking his friend to hold a horse. Instead, the idiom means to be patient. Can you identify any other

idioms in this book? (You can find one in Chapter 2!) What are some of the idioms that you and your friends use?

14. **Defining Moments**—Many good stories have defining moments. These moments could be life-changing and shocking events. In *Fires in the Wilderness*, the death of Jarek's brother, Squint, is one defining moment. Can you identify others?

15. **Misdirection**—Often, in storytelling, the author attempts to lead the reader to believe one thing, only to have events turn out differently. For example, Jarek is described as being a very good fighter who learned boxing skills from his father. Did you think that Jarek was going to win the boxing match against Mike O'Shea? Try writing a story that misdirects the reader to believe one thing, only to have events turn out differently.

16. **Messages**—Authors often insert messages into their stories reflecting their viewpoints and beliefs. In this book, one of the messages is that fighting doesn't solve problems. Can you identify any other messages?

17. **Symbolism**—The horror and danger of fire is symbolized as a beast. After Jarek saves Mike at the end of the story, the concluding paragraph begins with: "... the most terrible of all beasts had been conquered." What did the beast symbolize in this sentence? If you wanted to portray fire as something friendly, what symbol would you use?

18. **Title Selection**—Writers choose titles that will attract the reader and have a strong tie to the story. A good title shouldn't give away too much of the story or its outcome, yet it should provide an enticing hint into the storyline. The title for this book did not come easily to the author. Several ideas were rejected before finally settling on *Fires in the Wilderness*. What other titles would work for this story? Try to come up with three.

Acknowledgments

Thank you to John Gilmour, Al Hubbard, and the members of Chapter 129 of NACCCA/CCC Legacy of Grayling, Michigan, who gave their time and shared stories from their CCC days.

Thanks also are due to the many reviewers who poured over the manuscripts of this book: first and foremost, to my wife, Deborah; Harry Dallas, NACCCA Museum Director and enrollee; Sally McMullen; Janet Johnson; Ralph Schmidt; Byron Schatzer; and Piccola Sweebe.

Any errors of fact or misrepresentations are unintentional and solely the fault of the author.